PERSONAL JUSTICE

Rayven T. Hill

Ray of Joy Publishing
Toronto

Books by Rayven T. Hill

Blood and Justice
Cold Justice
Justice for Hire
Captive Justice
Justice Overdue
Justice Returns
Personal Justice
Silent Justice
Web of Justice
Fugitive Justice

Visit rayventhill.com for more information
on these and future releases.

Published by Ray of Joy Publishing
Toronto

ISBN-13: 978-0-9938625-6-4

PERSONAL JUSTICE

CHAPTER 1

DAY 1 - Monday, 7:12 p.m.

WERNER SHAFT drove through the gathering darkness, singing along with the radio, his head bobbing back and forth. His fingers tapped out a rhythm on the steering wheel as the first shot blasted a hole through the driver-side window. Unfortunately, Shaft wasn't destined to live long enough to appreciate the science behind the deflection of a bullet through glass, often causing it to miss its intended target.

Suffice it to say, the first bullet missed.

And so did the second. By then Shaft had hit the brakes with all his weight, causing the 2010 Corolla to spin fully around on the pavement, its headlights cutting through the late evening fog, now facing back toward the warehouse area of the city and the backbreaking job he had left but a few minutes before.

Though he heard the shot, the second projectile was lost somewhere in the darkness, its target no longer viable as

1

Shaft ducked down in the front seat. He frantically unlatched the passenger door and pushed it open with one hand while the other dug for a pistol held securely in place by an underarm holster.

The shot had come from the open window of another vehicle. He hadn't seen the danger, had never so much as glanced at the car in the lane beside him, never suspecting it held a killer.

He wormed out the open door, rolled to the ground, and crouched by the rear fender of his vehicle, his pistol cocked and ready to bring down the shooter.

His would-be assassin pulled over to the shoulder and stopped the car thirty feet ahead. Water vapor puffed from the tailpipe, red lights glowed from the rear, and the driver-side door hung open, the interior light of the now-empty vehicle splashing onto the pavement beside the car.

But the shooter was nowhere to be seen.

Shaft wished he'd stayed in his vehicle and tried a run for safety. His chances would've been better than what he now faced. Or rather, didn't face, because there was no indication where the would-be killer was hiding.

The third shot blasted its way through the taillight, inches from his head, sending shards of glass and metal to the ground at his feet.

He raised his weapon, poked his head around the shattered light, and chanced a glance to where the shot appeared to have come from. He saw no one. The muffler of his vehicle rumbled noisily beside him, the car engine still running, and he heard the distinct crackle of footsteps on loose gravel somewhere to his left.

2

He dove back the length of the vehicle, keeping low, and crawled to a safe spot at the front of the car. Safe for now, but for how long? He couldn't see his assailant, and perhaps there were more than one.

They'd caught up with him, coming to claim his life in lieu of the cash. Retribution.

He wondered if they had already gotten to Norton. Perhaps his partner was dead already. The whole thing was a fiasco from the beginning, but he had been certain they'd made good their escape nonetheless. Now he wasn't so sure.

A car whipped by, slowed a moment, and then sped off. Another car followed, both drivers unaware of the gunman stalking Shaft from somewhere in the darkness. The lack of streetlights was a detriment to his safety, putting him at a distinct disadvantage.

He licked his dry lips and wiped his brow with a free hand. He was sweating despite the chilly evening. His hand trembled and he wished he'd shut off the engine. Then he might have a chance of hearing his pursuer.

With his back to the front bumper, crouching low, he looked left, then right, each time swinging the pistol in rhythm with his head.

Where was the gunman?

Bullet number four grazed his shoulder as he made a dive for the sidewalk. He gritted his teeth and dashed over the patch of grass that separated the street from the adjoining building, a shoe store, now closed for the night.

Number five missed as his feet hit the gravel in the alleyway by the side of the shop. He heard running behind him. His pursuer was catching up. He stumbled once, caught himself, and ran headlong down the alley to the rear corner of the building.

He whipped around the corner, then spun back, leveled his weapon, peered around, and took a shot. He was shooting blind and must have missed the unseen target. He was never good with these things. The crunch on gravel continued and he fired again, dashing to his left. His only thought was to get as far away as possible.

A sudden panic overtook him as he dashed along the rear of the building. They'd tracked him this far, and they would track him forever, relentlessly pursuing him until he was dead.

He needed to run and never stop until he was out of the city, maybe the country—if he survived this night.

Shaft spun around a big blue dumpster at the rear of the building, narrowly missing it in the darkness. His shoulder was burning like crazy where the bullet entered, but that was the least of his worries. It could've been a leg, or worse. At least he could still run, and run he did, past the dumpster, around a parked car, all the while knowing his pursuer was mere seconds behind.

He spun on one heel, dropped to a crouch, then leveled his gun and squeezed the trigger.

No one was there. He heard a chuckle. Where was it coming from? Behind the dumpster, perhaps?

He straightened slowly and backed up, keeping his gun ready, finally reaching the far corner of the building.

It was another alleyway, leading back to the street, empty and bare. There would be no form of protection. He would need to be careful, and perhaps he might be lucky enough to make it the distance.

He backed into the alley, his weapon raised, ready at a

second's notice to pull the trigger. Step by step he retreated, watching, waiting, hoping to see the assassin step into his line of fire.

Except for the pistol shaking in his unsteady hand and the thumping of his heart, he felt tense and stiff. He could hardly breathe, managing short, quick breaths as he moved slowly toward a safer place.

Then from behind him, a footstep and a chuckle. The killer had retreated, circled the building, and now came at him from behind.

He cursed his own stupidity as bullet number six bit into his back, burrowed through his spinal cord, and entered his left lung.

He sank to the ground and lay flat on his destroyed back, shards of gravel biting the back of his head, his body numb, in shock, and his mind in turmoil.

He looked up at his murderer through dimming eyes. He saw a face, and a pistol grasped in a steady hand, its barrel aimed toward his skull, and then utter darkness as his eyesight faded to black.

Number seven had his name on it. The one destined to end his worthless life.

Werner Shaft took one last breath and spoke his final words, one second before bullet number seven left the assassin's gun and made its way into the inner recesses of his brain.

"It's you. Why?"

He didn't hear the answer, if perchance there was one.

CHAPTER 2

Monday, 7:49 p.m.

ANNIE LINCOLN shut down her computer and leaned back, the annoying squeak of her swivel chair again reminding her to ask Jake to give it a drop or two of oil. She could just as easily do it herself, but anything that remotely smacked of maintenance, Jake stubbornly claimed as his territory.

It was an unremarkable day. Cranston's Department Store had requested background checks on several prospective employees, a law firm needed some legal papers served ASAP, Richmond Insurance urgently wanted some research done, and the one that made her smile, a ten-year-old boy wanted to hire them to find a lost puppy. She'd politely declined that one.

Lincoln Investigations, the business she had started not so long ago with her husband, now flourished. In addition to their mainstay of research, more than their fair share of bad guys came their way. Their recent successes in apprehending criminals had led to a surge of publicity that couldn't be bought. With more business than they could handle, they were now in the position to pick and choose. It was exciting, often dangerous, and always demanding—but Annie loved it.

And so did Jake. He wouldn't go back to his old job as a construction engineer for twice the money he'd once received. After he was laid off some time ago, turning Annie's part-time research company into a full-fledged business had been his brainstorm. Annie had been skeptical at first, but now she wouldn't have it any other way. It turned out to be challenging, satisfying, and exhilarating. Working alongside her husband was a bonus.

She straightened up some stray papers on her desk, filed a couple of folders in a drawer, pushed back her chair—it squeaked again—and wandered into the adjoining living room. Jake sprawled on the floor, a pillow under his head, watching television. His six-foot-four-inch body stretched halfway across the room. He held the remote control in one hand, the other tucked behind his head.

A smaller copy of her husband lay beside him. Eight-year-old Matty was destined and determined to be like his father—both were somewhat reckless and impulsive at times, too cocky for their own good, and the best-looking guys Annie had ever seen. Matty was intent on the TV, his eyes wide as the program wound down.

She stopped in front of them and looked down at her son. "Matty, is your homework done?"

Matty didn't look up. "Aw, it's only math, Mom. I'll do it later. It's a snap."

"I think you should get at it now," Annie suggested firmly.

Jake turned his eyes her way. "Five minutes, okay? CSI is almost over. I'll make sure he gets it done." He turned his eyes back to the TV.

Annie relented, navigated past the guys, and gazed out the front window toward the street. The neighborhood was quiet. The sun was already set, final shades of red and orange barely visible on the horizon. She pulled the drapes closed, snuggled up in her easy chair, and reached for her book—a book on real crime scene investigation, not the one-hour TV version. She was always eager to increase her knowledge of investigative techniques and police procedure, and her library continued to expand as fast as she could devour the books.

Half a chapter later, the television was dark, Matty on his way upstairs, and Jake lounged on the couch. She felt him staring at her and she looked up. "Something on your mind?" she asked.

He shrugged. "Nothing more than usual. Just enjoying your company. Things have been busy lately and we haven't had a lot of quiet time."

"You could read a book," Annie said, glancing to one of two stuffed bookshelves flanking the fireplace. Reading was one of her passions and she couldn't understand why everyone didn't feel the same way.

"Maybe later," Jake said, and she knew he wouldn't. He crossed his arms and dropped his feet on the coffee table. "What's on the agenda for tomorrow?"

Annie shrugged. "You can look for a lost dog if you want to."

"A lost dog?"

"I really don't have anything for you right now."

"What kind of dog?"

Annie frowned. "I didn't ask. I turned it down."

"I had a dog once," Jake said, his brow wrinkled in thought. "When I was a boy we had this ugly-looking mutt. We called it 'Ugly' because it was." He paused and took a deep breath. "I loved that dog. Broke my heart when it died. Dad wanted to get me another one but nothing could ever replace Ugly."

"My mother never allowed a dog in the house. She said they were too messy." Annie chuckled. "But we had a cat. A real mean beast." She laughed out loud. "A bit like my mother. But Dad put up with it."

A grin appeared on Jake's face. "Like he puts up with your mother."

Annie shrugged. "Maybe she's getting better. She actually mentioned your name yesterday without having anything nasty to say about you."

Jake gave a short laugh. "Maybe it's me that's getting better."

Annie stood, went to the couch, and curled up beside her husband. She wrapped her arms around his neck and gave him an extended kiss. "I can't find any room for improvement," she said. "You seem fine to me."

He grinned and gave her another kiss. "You're a good influence on me. I can be bad when I want to."

"There's time for that later." She ran her fingers through his short dark hair and got off the couch, settling back in her easy chair, her feet curled underneath herself.

"Sounds like a good plan," Jake said, looking at his watch. "But right now, I have to give the other love of my life a rubdown. She gets lonely without me."

Annie laughed. She didn't mind playing second fiddle to a car. After all, it was a 1986 Pontiac Firebird, and even though she wasn't much for cars, she was first to admit it was a beautiful machine.

Jake stood. "I'll give it a quick polishing and be back soon. It got spotted from the rain this afternoon. Should've parked it in the garage."

"Bring back some oil with you."

"Oil?"

She pointed a thumb toward the office. "My chair squeaks."

He nodded and Annie watched him leave. She went to the kitchen, fixed herself a cup of hot chocolate, and carried it to the living room. She settled back into her chair, sipped the drink, and picked up her book. It was nice to have some peace and quiet for a change, just her and her family.

She grimaced when she heard a roar from the adjoining garage. Jake was warming up the Firebird. So much for the quiet, but at least it was still peaceful.

And peace was what she needed. The previous week had been a hectic nightmare, its frightening events still fresh in her mind, and she looked forward to a week without vicious killers, violent criminals, and treacherous thieves.

CHAPTER 3

Monday, 8:19 p.m.

FOR THE FIRST time in weeks, Detective Hank Corning had been able to leave work a few minutes early. Richmond Hill was growing, and his post as head of the small Canadian city's robbery/homicide division kept him busy as crime grew along with the city.

Hank had used the opportunity to take his ever-patient girlfriend, Amelia, out to an early dinner at Tommy Tomatto's, a little Italian buffet and one of their favorite places to dine. They had just returned to her house and snuggled up in front of the television when his cell phone rang.

Hank's deep-brown eyes narrowed at the news. There was a homicide, their tranquil evening interrupted.

He sighed and stood up, brushed a hand through his short-cropped hair, and called his sometime partner, Detective Simon King, arranging to meet him at the scene.

Though Hank preferred to work alone, his growing workload required him to depend more and more on King. The unkempt cop wouldn't have been Hank's first choice for a partner, but the captain had insisted.

The scene was a hub of activity as Hank approached. First responders had immediately cordoned off the street in front of a pair of shops. Three cruisers, their lights flashing, parked outside the yellow tape, the forensic van close by. Other cars were stopped at haphazard angles. Orange cones, wooden barriers, and a cop at each end of the area detoured the sparse traffic to other avenues.

An officer waved Hank through. He parked beside a cruiser and glanced across the street. King was already there, sitting in his vehicle. As Hank crossed over, the greasy-haired cop stepped out and shoved his hands into the pockets of his worn-out jeans. "What took you so long?"

Hank disregarded the question and turned toward the crime scene. A 2010 Corolla sat in the center of the taped-off area, parked awkwardly in the middle of the street, its passenger-side door hanging open. The interior light of the vehicle still shone, and its headlights cast streaks of white light down the asphalt. The engine was still running.

The empty vehicle stood in front of Master Footwear, a shoe store boasting half-price sales year round. Beside it, Nortown Bakery sat with a darkened interior, its backlit overhead sign glowing.

A narrow alleyway between the two shops was the center of attention. Remote area lighting was set up, bringing the brightness of daylight to the entire sealed-off area as well as the alley and the rear of the buildings.

Investigators processed the scene, a painstaking job and a massive undertaking considering the extent of the area.

It was going to be a long night for CSI.

The detectives approached lead crime scene investigator Rod Jameson. "Evening, Rod," Hank said and King grunted.

At six foot two, the investigator looked down a couple of inches at Hank and pointed toward the deserted car in the center of the street. A deep, hollow voice came out of his thin frame. "It looks like the action started over there"—he swung around and pointed to the alleyway—"and ended over there. The body's in that alley." He consulted a clipboard. "Victim has been IDed as Werner Shaft and this vehicle is registered in his name."

They followed him to the idling car. Hank circled around, taking note of the bullet hole in the driver-side window, the broken taillight, and the open passenger-side door.

King crouched down and examined the street. "Looky here, Hank."

Hank glanced to where the detective pointed.

King continued, "Those skid marks look fresh. It appears there might've been a second vehicle that made a quick stop, heading south." He pointed to the car. "And those skid marks indicate this one was heading south as well, then the driver hit the brakes and spun around."

"And the shooter was in the unknown vehicle," Hank said. "Makes sense."

"You can see by the skid marks, the vehicles were in adjoining lanes, probably side by side when the shot through the driver-side window occurred."

"Then the victim stopped quick and spun around," Hank said. "He then exited through the passenger door in an attempt to get away, leaving the vehicle running."

"And the assailant stopped a few feet later."

Hank brought King's attention to the broken taillight. "It looks like a shoot-out ensued, then the victim ran across the street and down the alley."

"He didn't get far," Rod said. "The victim was shot three times. There's no way to tell how many might've missed their target."

"We'd better go take a look," Hank said.

The medical examiner, Nancy Pietek, had finished her preliminary examination when Hank and King approached the body of the victim.

Nancy turned her always cheerful round face upwards. "It's another lovely evening, Hank."

"Wonderful," Hank said and looked down at the body. It lay face up, a gaping wound in the middle of the forehead. Blood pooled under the abdomen and soaked into the gravel below. A semiautomatic pistol lay near his right hand.

"What can you tell me, Nancy?"

Nancy stood up, straightening her short, pleasantly rounded frame, and craned her neck up at Hank. "It appears the cause of death was a GSW to the head by a small-caliber weapon. Gunshot residue on the victim indicates it was fired from a distance of eighteen to twenty-four inches. No more than that."

"So the killer was face to face with the victim when he fired the final shot," Hank said.

"It appears so," Nancy said, turning her eyes back to the body. "There are also two more gunshot wounds, one to the left shoulder, entering the deltoid muscle from the rear at approximately a forty-five-degree angle. Exited at the front. Not fatal. No residue."

"And the other?" Hank asked.

Nancy crouched again and rolled the body halfway over. She pointed to a large blood-covered area at the back of the victim's shirt. "GSW here, almost dead center of the back, through the spinal cord. There's no exit wound, so the bullet's probably lodged somewhere inside the body, possible in the lung or heart area."

Hank crouched down beside Nancy. "Gunshot residue?"

"No. No residue, but given the area and severity of the wound, a shot like that would've brought him down."

Hank pulled a rubber glove from his pocket and put it on. He picked up the pistol that lay by the victim, held it close to his nose, and announced, "It's been fired recently. The victim tried to defend himself. Obviously, unsuccessfully."

Nancy agreed. "Gunshot residue on the victim's right hand will confirm that."

Hank put the weapon back down, stood up, and considered the medical evidence. "The fact there's residue on the shot to the forehead, appears to have made that the final wound of the three. There would be no need to shoot the victim in the back after he's already dead." He scratched his head. "Looks like the victim was already on the ground when the final shot was taken."

King added, "The killer chased the victim into the alley,

wounding him in the shoulder first, then bringing him down with a shot to the back."

"And then he finished him off with a bullet to the head," Hank said.

"It appears that way," Nancy said as she stood. "The body wasn't moved after death. The victim died right here. I expect you'll find the bullet embedded in the gravel under the head once they take a look."

"Time of death?" King asked.

"One to two hours ago," Nancy said, pointing toward the street. "Apparently, there's a witness."

Hank raised his brows. "A witness?"

Nancy nodded. "A man—on his way home from work. He's waiting out front. I believe an officer is taking his statement."

"We have the cause of death and the victim's name," Hank said. "That's the easy part. All we need now is a motive and a perpetrator." He nudged King toward the street. "Let's go see what the witness can tell us."

CHAPTER 4

Monday, 8:44 p.m.

HANK AND KING were directed to the witness waiting patiently on a bench outside the taped-off area. Earlier, the man had given his name to one of the officers as Victor Stone.

"I apologize for keeping you waiting, Mr. Stone," Hank said, offering his hand and introducing himself and King as they approached.

Stone rose to his feet, shook the detective's hand, and nodded at King. "I don't mind waiting. I'm only too happy to help."

Hank reached into an inner pocket of his jacket, removed a well-used notepad and pen, and thumbed to a blank page. He made a notation and looked at the witness.

Stone was middle-aged, a patch of gray around his temples, the rest of his head covered by a baseball cap. An ever-smiling mouth, even when he talked, gave his face a somewhat eerie appearance, especially when coupled with a frown. His slim body slouched forward at the shoulders, his blue eyes on Hank, as he tucked his hands into the pockets of his faded jeans and spoke. "I've never seen anything like this before. It's rather unnerving."

"It certainly would be," Hank said with an understanding nod and an encouraging smile. "I'll make this as quick as possible. I need to know exactly what you saw."

Stone took a deep breath and pointed across the street. "I was on my way home from work—I only live a few blocks away, so I walk. I was minding my own business, not paying any attention to traffic, when I heard a gunshot, and a car squealed to a stop behind me."

King interrupted. "Which car?"

"Actually, it must've been both cars," Stone said, pointing to the Corolla in the middle of the street. "When I turned, that one was already spun around like that, but another one was stopped a little closer to me."

"Can you describe the second car?" Hank asked.

Stone nodded. "It was a white Honda Accord. Not sure what year. Recent."

"Plate?"

"I didn't think to check the plate. I dove off the sidewalk out of sight behind a tree. If there was shooting going on, I didn't want to be part of it."

"Of course," Hank said. "That's the sensible thing to do." He made a note in his pad and looked back up. "Then what happened?"

"The driver of this car," Stone said, pointing to the

Corolla, "crawled out the passenger door and the other guy got out of his car. Then they started shooting at each other. The dead guy ran around to the front of his car, then crossed the street and ran up beside that building."

Hank looked to where Stone indicated. "He ran past the shoe store?" That was somewhat different from what he had presumed took place.

"Yes, he ran up there and the other guy followed. I heard two shots, and then the killer ran back this way and into the alleyway between the two stores."

Hank looked toward the alley. According to Stone, the victim went around the shoe store and the shooter circled back and cut him off. "You're sure that's how it happened?"

Stone nodded his head adamantly. "Absolutely sure."

"And then?"

"Then I heard two or three more shots. Not sure how many. Then the killer ran from the alley, got into his car, and left."

"Can you describe the shooter?"

"It was pretty dark, but when he got out of the car, I saw he wore a plaid shirt. Red. Dark pants. A baseball cap." He paused. "That's about all I saw."

"How tall?" King asked.

Stone shrugged. "Regular height, I guess. Not especially tall or short. I wasn't paying a lot of attention to that. It all happened quickly."

"Could you make out any facial features?" Hank asked.

"No. Like I said, it was dark."

"Did either one of them speak at any time?"

Stone shook his head. "Not that I heard."

Hank looked at Detective King. "Anything else?"

King shrugged a shoulder. "Did you notice what time it happened?"

Stone frowned and looked at the ground, thinking out loud. "I got off work at seven, and it would've been shortly after that." He looked at King. "Maybe seven ten or seven fifteen at the latest."

Hank made a notation, closed the pad, and tucked it back into his pocket, then removed a business card and handed it to Stone. "Give me a call if you think of anything else."

Stone took the card, looked at it briefly, and put it into his back pocket.

"Do you want a lift home?" Hank asked.

"I'll be fine," Stone said, pointing over his shoulder. "I don't live far."

Hank thanked him and he and King ducked back under the tape and went to where Rod Jameson stood. Hank told the lead investigator how the chase had gone down. "Make sure you check all the way around the shoe store for any trace evidence."

"Will do."

Hank turned to King. "That's about all we're going to get from here. You might as well go home. I'll go back to the precinct. There're a few things I need to check out, and then I'll see if Shaft has any family. I might need to make a visit."

"See you tomorrow, Hank," King said without hesitation and strode to his vehicle.

Though Hank always hated the uncomfortable task of

notifying a family of their loved one's death, he would sooner King wasn't there. The crass detective's manner wasn't something Hank wanted to subject them to if it could be helped.

Hank got in his car and drove to the precinct. He had a few errands that couldn't wait until morning.

The too-small room at RHPD was a hub of activity when Hank arrived. A drug bust had gone down in the early evening, and handcuffed suspects paraded through on their way to interview rooms or jail cells.

"Ten kilos of coke, all ready for the streets," Captain Diego informed him as Hank cut his way through the noise.

He blocked out the commotion and pulled up at his desk. A quick database search returned the personal information on Werner Shaft, complete with a picture. He would have to get Callaway to do a thorough background search later, but right now, it appeared Shaft was married, no kids. His wife's name was Maria, same phone number as her husband—probably a landline.

He printed the information, then dialed the listed number and waited. It rang several times. No answering machine kicked in, so Hank hung up. He would try again before he left for home.

He called Amelia, gave his apologies, wished her sweet dreams, and said he would talk to her in the morning. He wondered how long she would put up with his crazy hours, never knowing when he would be called in, or when he would get off.

Another computer search netted him phone numbers for

the managers of the two stores near the crime scene, Nortown Bakery and Master Footwear. Both managers informed him their respective shops had been closed, with no one in the buildings during the time in question. Neither had any cameras installed outside the property, so that was a dead end.

He wrote a note for Callaway, the technical wiz everyone depended on to set up wire taps or traces, or when they needed a thorough background check done on a suspect or person of interest. He dropped the note on Callaway's desk, where he would be sure to see it first thing.

After checking out the witness's story with his place of employment, Hank went over his notes. He didn't have much to start with. The description of the car was too vague. Another phone call to Maria Shaft had gone unanswered, and the CSI report would be awhile, so there was little else to do.

He shut down his computer, pushed back from his desk, and made his way back through the hubbub, heading for home.

CHAPTER 5

DAY 2 - Tuesday, 8:20 a.m.

JAKE STEPPED OFF the treadmill, wiped his brow, and did some dynamic stretches to cool down. The intense thirty-minute workout he went through each morning always made him feel refreshed, prepared for anything.

He went to the kitchen, downed almost a quart of water, took a quick shower, and dressed. Now he was ready.

Annie and Matty were in the kitchen when he came back downstairs. Matty popped the last bite of toast into his mouth, finished his orange juice, and pushed back his plate. He sighed, a troubled look on his face. "Guess I'd better get to school."

Annie turned away from the sink, sat at the table, and looked at Matty. "Is something wrong?"

He sighed again. "Not really."

"Did something happen at school?"

Matty looked at his mother, then shrugged and turned away, pushing back his chair.

Annie put a hand on Matty's shoulder as he tried to stand. "Sit down, Matty. Tell me what's wrong."

Jake sat and leaned his arms on the table.

"Aw, Mom. You wouldn't understand," Matty said, his shoulders slumped.

"Try me."

Matty raised his eyes. "It's the girls, Mom."

"The girls?"

"They won't leave me alone. They think I'm some kind of hero because of what happened up north, and they keep hanging around."

Jake laughed. "That's a terrible problem."

Matty looked at his father, disgust on his face. "I don't want no girls hanging around all the time. All the guys think I'm a sissy."

Annie ignored the bad grammar and chuckled. "The other boys are jealous, that's all."

Matty frowned. "You think so, Mom?"

"I'm sure of it."

"You'll just have to deal with it, son," Jake said. "It happened to me when I was your age. Get used to it."

Annie gave Jake a dry look and rolled her eyes. "Your dad is right. Well, half right. You have to put up with it and they'll leave you alone after a while."

Matty nodded, got up, and went to the fridge. He retrieved his lunch and stuffed it into his backpack. "Guess I'll get going."

"Brush your teeth first," Annie said.

"Yes, Mom." Matty dropped the pack on his shoulder and walked slowly from the kitchen.

Jake looked at Annie, a twinkle in his eye. "Matty doesn't know how lucky he is."

"Every girl loves a hero," Annie said. "And I've found mine." She stood, picked up Matty's dishes, and put them in the sink. "I've got work to do." She washed her hands and headed to the office.

The front door opened and closed; Matty was off to school. Jake washed up the dishes, put them away, and went to the office. He dropped into a chair and stretched out his long legs.

Annie hung up the phone. "That was Chris," she said. "From Cranston's."

Cranston's Department Store was the anchor of the busiest mall in the area, and the retail giant occasionally turned work toward Lincoln Investigations. Chris, as head of security, had once complained to them how his department was underfunded. The owners of the store preferred to maintain a skeleton security staff and farm out work to independents if unusual circumstances demanded it.

"What does Chris need this time?" Jake asked.

"It seems like they've had a rash of shoplifters lately. Chris feels it's more than that. It's his opinion Cranston's is being targeted by an organized retail crime ring."

"Shoplifting networks have always existed," Jake said. "I don't mean your occasional person who lifts a pair of pants, or a CD. I'm talking about professionals who hit the easiest targets. Cranston's needs to beef up security. They'll never put a stop to it, but they can deter it."

"Perhaps you're right, but I think we should go and see

Chris," Annie said. "We have no other major tasks at the moment."

"I'm ready."

Annie called Chris back, and fifteen minutes later, Jake tapped on the door of Cranston's security office, located on the main floor of the massive store.

"Come in."

A burly man in his late twenties rose from his desk when Jake pushed the door open. He and Annie stepped in. The man leaned over his small desk and offered a hand and a huge grin. "Welcome, guys."

Jake shook his hand and Chris motioned toward a pair of chairs. "Sit."

Annie sat and crossed her legs while Jake dropped into his and stretched out, folding his arms. "We're happy to help out, Chris," Jake said. "But I think all you people need is more security personnel."

Chris leaned forward at his desk. "I told them that, but they aren't willing to shell out the cash on an ongoing basis. Gave me the long lecture about how shoplifting is part of the cost of doing business."

"That's true," Annie said. "But you gave me the indication it's unusually high right now."

"It is. It is." Chris rubbed the stubble on his chin. "We've either been proved to be an easy mark, or we're being targeted by a shoplifting ring."

"Or both," Jake said. "Likely both."

"Richmond Hill PD has no organized crime unit," Annie said. "I believe it falls under the jurisdiction of burglary, and they're overworked and understaffed. The police don't have the time or the resources to handle every case of shoplifting."

"So what's the answer?" Chris asked. "You guys can't curb it by yourselves, and my staff is too small to make much of a dent. They don't want to put guards at every door. It makes the shoppers feel uneasy, and that's bad for business."

"We have to pull it up by the roots," Jake said.

"What does that mean?"

Jake stood and paced the small office, speaking as he thought. "If this is a ring, there's no point in grabbing the occasional booster. They'll just be replaced." He stood still and looked at Chris. "We have to get to the ringleaders—to the fences, the ones who're receiving and redistributing the stolen goods."

"It's not just Cranston's," Chris said. "Every store goes through this at one time or another. We catch a lot of shoplifters, but the professional boosters are probably getting away."

"What about your cameras?" Jake asked.

Chris shook his head slowly. "These people are a different breed of thieves. Cameras often identify the casual shoplifter, but the organized boosters are more brazen. They often disguise themselves in some way, or avoid the cameras altogether."

"Or they wait until no one's paying attention and they walk out," Annie said.

"Exactly. But if they're seen, and even if the security tags go off at the door, cashiers and clerks do little to stop them and usually let them run. Sometimes they call the police, but by then, they're gone." Chris shrugged and let out a long breath. "I can't blame them. Who wants to risk getting injured for minimum wage?"

Annie sat forward. "Leave it with us, Chris. We'll work on it and see if we can come up with a plan of action. We might not zero in on the ringleaders, but we'll see what we can do for Cranston's."

Chris grinned. "You have an idea?"

Jake looked at Annie. "We're working on it." He didn't have any great plan yet, but he knew between the two of them, they'd figure something out.

Jake stood, shook Chris's hand, and followed Annie through the store and back out to the parking lot. "Any ideas?" he asked, as they got in the Firebird.

"Nothing yet," Annie said.

CHAPTER 6

Tuesday, 9:05 a.m.

HANK SAT AT THE kitchen table in his small apartment. His pushed his breakfast dishes aside and sipped at a coffee as he reviewed his scant notes regarding the murder of Werner Shaft.

Callaway hadn't had time to take care of Hank's request, and CSI still had nothing for him, so he submitted to the inevitable and made another phone call to Maria Shaft.

This time, there was an answer.

Hank introduced himself and asked if he could drop by to see her right away.

He heard Mrs. Shaft take a quick breath. There was a pause, and then, "Is … is this to do with my husband? He didn't come home last night and I'm out of my mind."

This was not something Hank wanted to do over the phone. He needed to see her in person. "Mrs. Shaft, I'll be there in fifteen minutes." He double-checked the address he'd found for Werner Shaft, was assured it was correct, and hung up the phone. He grabbed his briefcase and keys, strapped on his service weapon, and went to his car.

Hank usually enjoyed his job, but the task he now faced was one he dreaded. As he drove, he thought about the many times in the past he'd had to do this very same thing, and it always went the same way—denial, anger, acceptance, then mourning. And for him, it never got any easier.

The only positive aspect was the motivation it gave him to catch the culprit, and a determination to persevere until they were brought to justice.

The Shaft residence was located in a middle-class neighborhood on a mature street. There was nothing outstanding about the brick dwelling itself—a double-car garage in front, the odd plant and shrub scattered around, one car in the driveway.

He parked behind a dark green Mazda, got out of his car, and went up the brick pathway to the front door. He took a deep breath and rang the bell.

Maria Shaft was in her midthirties, with long dark hair and a roundish face. When she answered the door, Hank saw lines of worry on her face, her unsmiling mouth set in a grim line.

He introduced himself and she showed him to the front room. He sat uneasily on the couch as she took a seat in a matching chair. She leaned forward slightly, her hands in her lap. "Has my husband done something he shouldn't have, Detective? He's been arrested again, hasn't he?"

Hank gathered his thoughts as he placed his briefcase carefully on the cushion beside him and sat back. He took a deep breath and observed her closely. "I'm afraid it's more than that."

She tilted her head slightly to one side, the expression on her face unchanged.

"Your husband was killed last night, Mrs. Shaft."

Her eyes widened, her mouth opened, and she remained still a moment, then, "Killed? How? Are you sure it was him?"

Hank snapped open his briefcase, removed the printout on Werner Shaft, and held it up for her to see. "Is this your husband, ma'am?"

She nodded. "Yes."

Hank put the paper back in his briefcase. "There's no mistake. It was him."

She stared at Hank, her breathing quick and erratic. Then in a hoarse voice, barely above a whisper, she asked, "What happened?"

"He was murdered."

Her eyes opened wider. "Murdered?"

"I'm afraid so, ma'am. I'm sorry. I tried to reach you last night."

"I was babysitting," she whispered. "For my sister. I wasn't home until late." She paused. "Do you know who ... killed him?"

"Not yet," Hank said. "If you're up to it, I need to ask you a few questions."

She nodded and reached to the stand near her chair for a tissue. The tears started, and she dabbed at her eyes, sobbing quietly.

"Do you know of anyone who might've wanted to harm your husband?"

She hesitated and glanced aside. Finally, she looked Hank in the eye and said, "Detective, my husband was involved with some bad characters in the past. As you probably know, he did some time in prison, but I ... I didn't know any of his former acquaintances. Perhaps someone he knew before ..."

That caught Hank by surprise. He hadn't had the time to dig very deeply, still unaware of Werner Shaft's record. That opened it up to a lot of possibilities, and it also might explain why Shaft carried a weapon.

"We've just started the investigation, Mrs. Shaft, so we have no suspects yet. Anything you can tell us might help."

Maria Shaft sniffed and wiped at her nose. "I'll help you with whatever you want to know, but I'm at a loss."

Hank pulled out his notepad and pen and cleared his throat. "Do you and your husband have any children?"

"No, we never did." She looked away wistfully. "Werner never wanted children and so ..." Her voice trailed off, leaving Hank with the impression she'd begrudgingly yielded to her husband's wishes.

Hank made a notation in his pad. "So, it's just the two of you here?"

Mrs. Shaft leaned forward. "My husband's brother lives with us. Rocky. He occupies the basement apartment."

Hank made another note. "Do you know if he's home right now?"

She shook her head. "He works at the same place my husband works ... worked. He'll be there now."

"And where's that?"

"Werner was the warehouse manager at Richmond Distributing, and Rocky works in the shipping department."

Hank wrote down the name and put a question mark beside it. "Do they ride to work together?"

"Sometimes. It depends on their shift. This morning Rocky took his own vehicle because my husband ..."

"What kind of vehicle does Rocky drive?"

"It's a red Ford pickup. I'm not sure what year it is."

Hank nodded and made a note to find out what vehicle or vehicles were registered in Rocky's name. According to the witness, the killer had driven a white Honda Accord, and Hank wanted to find out if anyone close to Werner Shaft had a vehicle with that description registered in their name.

Another part of this uncomfortable task was asking uncomfortable questions. "Mrs. Shaft, you said you were babysitting last night for your sister. I'll need her name and address."

Mrs. Shaft didn't blink, perhaps not realizing Hank's intention was to check her alibi. "Her name's Melinda Windsor. They live at 335 Polimer Street." She paused. "Detective, you don't think they had anything to do with this, do you?"

"Not at all," Hank said, jotting down the information. "I just need to fill in all the pieces." He looked back up. "What time did you get home last night?"

"It was after eleven."

"Did you drive there?"

"Yes, I took my car."

Hank pointed over his shoulder. "The car in the driveway?"

"Yes."

Hank made a final note, read through what he wrote, and tucked his notepad away. He removed a card from his briefcase, leaned over, and handed it to the grieving widow. "Call me if you think of anything that might be useful."

"I will, Detective." She dabbed at her eyes with the tissue, took the card, and laid it on the stand beside her.

Hank stood, wished her well, and offered to connect her with their grief counseling services.

She declined the invitation and let him out.

He got into his car and looked at his notes. He had a few people to visit and some phone calls to make. He would assign the least sensitive ones to King and look after the rest himself.

Right now, he was anxious to see what Callaway had come up with.

CHAPTER 7

Tuesday, 9:18 a.m.

ANNIE AND JAKE sat in the Firebird in front of Cranston's, tossing around ideas. There were several approaches they could take in this situation, all of them viable.

"We could wait for somebody to boost something, follow them, and find out who they're selling to," was Jake's first suggestion.

Annie considered that a moment. "We need to get the top dog. A booster would likely be selling the stuff to a midlevel person, probably in some obscure location, and then it would be turned over to the top-level fence."

"If we can find the midlevel guy, can't we follow him?"

"Perhaps," Annie said. "But if this is as organized as I think, there's a lot of money involved, so there'll be a lot more security between the mid and top levels. I'm sure they take extreme precautions, and it's unlikely more than a few people know who runs the show or where the merchandise is warehoused."

Jake drummed his fingers on the steering wheel. "That's true. Boosters, and perhaps midlevel fences, get caught all the time, and the top dogs don't want to risk their operation whenever someone gets nabbed."

"There might be a better way," Annie said. "Most of this stuff is probably being sold at discount stores and flea markets. If we can find out who's selling stolen goods, we might be able to find out where they get it from."

"I don't think they'll give up their source to a couple of strangers," Jake said.

"What if we made a special order? Perhaps a quantity of something they sell and wait for a delivery?"

"And follow the delivery guy? That could mean staking out the place for hours, maybe days."

Annie's face twisted into a grimace. "Sounds like a long shot, doesn't it?"

Jake snapped his fingers and turned in his seat to face Annie. "I've got it," he said.

"Don't keep me in suspense."

Jake grinned. "Our goal is to follow the boosted goods to the final buyer, right?"

"Right."

"Simple." Jake shrugged a shoulder. "We put a tracker in the goods and see where they end up."

"And how do we know what they're going to boost?"

"Ah, that's the beauty of it. We set up a sting."

Annie thought a moment and then chuckled. "We tempt them with something they can't resist."

Jake nodded vigorously. "Exactly. What do you think?"

"It's the best idea yet and I think it's worth a shot. Let's go talk to Chris."

The security office was empty when Jake pushed the door open. They paged Chris from the nearby information desk. He soon showed up, a big grin splitting his face. "Back so soon? Did you solve the mystery of the disappearing stuff?"

Jake laughed. "Not yet, but we have an idea."

Chris waved toward the office and they went in and sat down.

"We want to set up a sting," Jake said. "We'll use a tracker and follow it."

"A sting?" Chris said. His eyes narrowed and Annie saw his mind considering it.

"You can catch more flies with honey than with vinegar," Annie said. "Boosters can't resist big-screen TVs."

Chris sat forward, rested his elbows on the desk, and cupped his hands under his bristly chin. He looked at Annie over top. "I think we can do that. I'll have to clear it with the manager, but I'm sure he'll go along with the game."

"We'll need his cooperation anyway," Jake said. "We need to make sure the goods with the trackers inside are too tempting to resist."

"I'm sure it can be arranged." Chris picked up the phone and paged the manager. In a few minutes, a fifty-something man entered the office. Jake explained the plan and was assured of full backing.

"He's under some heat from the owners as well," Chris said when the manager left. "I fully expected he'd be all for it." He stood. "I'm ready to get this thing underway as soon as you are."

"Let's do it," Jake said.

"I want to take a look around," Annie said as she stood. Jake and Chris followed her to the electronics department. A stack of big-screen televisions was on sale. "Those are perfect," she said. "Put them by the entrance door, not the exit. I want them to be seen when our mark comes in."

"I'll get the tracker," Jake said, turning to go. "It's in the car."

Chris pushed his cap back far enough to scratch his head. "What happens if we make this so tempting we end up turning an innocent shopper into a booster?"

Annie frowned at Chris. "So-called innocent shoppers don't become shoplifters unless it's in them to start with."

"Yeah, you're probably right, but what if a casual shoplifter takes it? One who's not associated with the organized ring?"

"That's a chance we'll have to take. If it happens, we'll bust the shoplifter, get the TV and tracker back, and try again."

"Kill two birds with one stone."

"Let's hope we'll kill more than two."

Jake sauntered back in and handed a small metal box to Chris. "Here's the tracker. All set up and ready to go. Put this in the case with the TV and we're good. We can track its location on my cell phone at any time." Jake pulled out his phone and revealed a web-based map. A red dot on the map indicated the tracker's current location.

"Excellent," Chris said. "I'll get a stock boy to set it up immediately."

Within ten minutes, an inventory control clerk wheeled a dolly of cartons to the designated spot. Jake carefully opened one, inserted the tracker deep inside the packaging where it wouldn't be seen if opened, then seamlessly taped it closed.

Just inside the front door, below a display model, the stack of televisions was set up, the box with the tracker on top.

"Perfect," Jake said. "It's motion activated, so we'll know exactly when the box is moved. Now we wait." He turned to Chris. "Make sure none of the security personnel hang around the front door. We don't want to scare anyone off."

"I'll get on it right away," Chris said as he turned to go. "Ring me as soon as something happens."

"Oh, one more thing," Annie said.

Chris turned back.

"Make sure nobody buys the top one. We don't want the police to break down the door of one of your customers."

Chris laughed. "Yeah, that wouldn't be good for business." He waved a hand and was gone.

Jake and Annie went to the Firebird and Jake pulled the vehicle into a spot closer to the front of the building. They had a direct view of the merchandise. He opened the trunk, retrieved two pairs of binoculars from a cardboard box, got back in the car, and handed one pair to Annie.

Annie adjusted the focus, training her binoculars on the front window. She could see perfectly.

All they needed to do now was wait.

CHAPTER 8

Tuesday, 9:54 a.m.

HANK PAID A VISIT to Melinda Windsor before returning to the precinct. Mrs. Windsor confirmed her sister, Maria Shaft, had been babysitting for her the previous evening, from 7:00 until 11:00 pm. Mrs. Windsor and her husband had gone out for the evening for dinner and a movie. They'd gotten back not long before 11:00 p.m., and Mrs. Shaft had driven herself home at that time. That fit with the story Maria Shaft had given him.

At the time of the shooting of Werner Shaft, Maria Shaft had indeed been babysitting.

The Windsors weren't suspects, but for the sake of being thorough, he checked their alibi. The waiter at the restaurant remembered them. He confirmed they were there when the murder took place. The time span of the movie was well past the time of the incident, so was inconsequential.

He drove to the precinct, mulling over what he knew. He

had little at this point, the victim's car being the best piece of evidence. He still needed to get the forensic report, which might give him something to go on, and, less likely to be of help, the ME's report. Both should be available later today, but he made a note to check with CSI.

He parked his Chevy in the back lot, rounded the building, and went up the set of steps to the RHPD precinct. When he stepped inside, he was relieved to find it was a lot quieter than the evening before. The drug squad had finished congratulating each other on the prior day's bust and was settled in to work on their next undertaking.

Everything was back to normal—whatever normal was.

Detective King moped around, perhaps jealous he'd been removed from the drug squad to work homicide as Hank's partner. Hank wasn't sure what Diego's thinking was on that decision. Perhaps he wanted to see where King worked best. Hank's opinion was King didn't fit in comfortably anywhere except maybe the occasional undercover job. He fit in pretty well with a lot of the riffraff on the streets, with a way—that Hank frowned on—of getting information from the criminal element.

Hank set his briefcase beside his chair and crossed the precinct floor to Officer Callaway's desk. The young cop glanced up as Hank approached and slid a file folder over, handing it to the detective.

"Some interesting stuff on Werner Shaft there for you. He's got a record."

"Thanks, Callaway." Hank took the folder back to his desk and sat, pulling his chair in.

He opened the folder and studied its contents. Werner Shaft was an ex-con. He'd served time for burglary several years ago and had a short record before that, but he'd been clean since being released from prison. Shaft had either gone straight, or gone smart and never got caught.

Either way, he was dead now, and his record might have something to do with it.

Shaft's accomplice in the burglary case was another ex-con by the name of Michael Norton, also with no record since his release. There was no further information on Norton, Callaway's report concentrating on Shaft.

Hank spun his chair around and wheeled over to Callaway's desk. "If you have a minute to spare, I need a complete file on Michael Norton."

"Right away, Hank."

Back at his desk, Hank perused Shaft's file more thoroughly. As Maria had said, he was employed at Richmond Distributing. Hank made a note to drop by there and talk to some of his coworkers.

Callaway dropped a sheet of paper on Hank's desk. "Here's everything I could find on Norton."

Hank scrutinized the paper, flipped it over, ran his finger down the page, and stopped. Norton owned a 2012 Honda Accord registered in his name—white. It fit the description of the vehicle the gunman drove, according to the witness.

That information, along with his association with Shaft, was enough for them to bring Norton in, and maybe some serious questioning would result in a confession.

Hank got on the phone and called lead CSI Rod Jameson. "Do you have anything for me yet?"

"We're still processing everything, Hank," Rod said. "I just got the ballistics report back and I'll get it to you right away."

"Anything enlightening in there?" Hank asked.

"Not much. Gunman used a thirty-eight-caliber. We recovered ballistic evidence in the ground under the victim's head and ran it through our ID system. It turned up negative, so it wasn't used in a crime before as far as our system could tell. That doesn't mean it wasn't, it's just not in our system."

"Anything else?"

"We found some shell casings on the street as well as a handful in places around the buildings. We'll detail that for you and include it."

"Any prints anywhere?"

"It doesn't look like it." Hank heard the rustle of papers over the line. Jameson continued, "I'll get the ballistics report up to you right away and our complete report as soon as we get it finished. Our guys were up most of the night on this one and they're still hard at it."

"Let me know if you run across anything interesting in the meantime."

"Will do, Hank."

The shell casings seemed to confirm the witness's story—the victim had been chased around the building before getting killed between the two shops. Hank was interested in seeing the final report, which would detail exactly where those casings were found.

He didn't have a motive yet, but he presumed it was a revenge killing, or perhaps something to do with money. It usually was. There didn't seem to be any hard proof to connect Michael Norton to the shooting, but certainly probable cause. Enough for a search warrant.

Hank put together the written statement he would need for the warrant, explaining the crime Norton was suspected of committing, how it had been carried out, and what they expected to find in the search. He stuffed it into a file folder and went to his reluctant partner's desk. King sat with his chair tilted back on two legs, his feet on his cluttered desk. He crossed his arms and watched curiously as Hank approached.

"We have enough for a search warrant," Hank said. "Get off your lazy butt. Let's go get the warrant and we'll bring this guy in for questioning as well."

"Who's the perp?"

Hank dropped the folder in front of King. "Michael Norton."

King browsed the paperwork and whistled. "Looks convincing to me. That didn't take you long."

"All you have to do is apply yourself, King. It's not that hard. You should try it sometime."

King smirked. "I'm not so good at filling out reports, but I do my part." He slid his feet off the desk. The wheels of the chair hit the floor with a clunk as he stood. "Let's get him."

CHAPTER 9

Tuesday, 10:16 a.m.

JAKE AND ANNIE sat in the Firebird taking turns watching the merchandise through the binoculars. Several people had shown interest in the televisions. One had been sold, and the clerk had been careful to select the second carton in the stack.

Jake sat with the seat pushed back, his hands behind his head, his eyes closed, while Annie took her stint at surveillance.

"We might have a live one," she said at last.

Jake sat up and opened his eyes.

Annie dropped her glasses in her lap, leaned forward in the seat, and pointed to a red Hyundai hatchback sitting outside the front door of the store. "A guy in a hoodie got out of that vehicle a second ago. He left the car door open, opened the trunk, and went into the store. The driver's waiting."

Jake grabbed his binoculars and trained them on the store. A hoodie covered most of the man's face as he stood in front of the stack of TVs. Jake glanced toward the checkouts. The clerks were busy with customers. They watched the man spin around casually, then he picked up the top two cartons, hoisted one onto each shoulder, and strode from the store without a look back.

The man slid the cartons into the trunk, slammed the lid, and jumped into the front seat, and the car sped away as the front door closed.

Jake looked at Annie and grinned. "It's definitely a live one." He grabbed his iPhone and booted up the web-based map. A small red dot moved away from their current position. He handed the phone to Annie. "Let's see where he goes. You can navigate."

"Keep back," Annie said. "We don't want to be seen. All that matters is where he ends up."

Jake started the Firebird, backed from the slot, and zipped across the parking lot. As they approached the street, Annie kept her eyes on the map and pointed to the right. "He's that way about two blocks."

Jake turned and followed, making sure to keep a safe distance between him and the fleeing boosters. Jake lost track of him before long, but Annie guided him back on the right route. Five minutes later, after several turns, Annie held up the phone. The small red dot was at a standstill.

"It stopped," she said and pointed. "Turn there."

Jake slowed and turned the wheel. "If we knew we were going to be following someone, we could've brought your car. It would be invisible anywhere. This thing is as obvious as a pimple on the tip of your nose."

"You're comparing your car to a zit?"

"Okay, bad analogy."

"You'd better pull over here," Annie said. "He stopped right up there."

Jake pulled to the curb and stopped, picked up the binoculars, and trained them down the street. The Hyundai was pulled into the driveway of a house half a block away.

A few minutes later, a white van backed in behind the Hyundai.

"They must've called their connection on the way," Jake said. "It looks like they're about to make an exchange."

Jake and Annie watched through the binoculars as a man jumped from the van and opened the side door. The guys from the car stepped out and opened the trunk, and a booster began to transfer the stolen televisions to the van.

The other booster opened the garage door and spent the next few minutes carrying cartons and bags to the van.

"There's a whole treasure trove of stuff in there," Annie said.

"These guys are professionals. Those boxes probably hold everything from detergent, to cologne, to high-end electronics. And at ten cents on the dollar, a van full of stuff can add up pretty quickly."

The driver of the van inspected the contents of each container as it was loaded, jotting something in a notepad.

"We should've brought the camera," Jake said.

"I didn't know we'd get into this so soon or I would've."

"Doesn't matter. As long as the tracker's in there, we'll get them."

"He's counting out some bills," Annie said. "That guy must know his prices pretty well."

"This is likely all he does. It's his job to know prices."

The money was handed to one of the boosters. There was a lively discussion and the van driver peeled off a couple more bills and handed them over. He slammed the side door of the van, climbed in behind the steering wheel, and drove away.

The red dot on the cell phone began to move.

Jake set the binoculars down and turned to Annie. "Phase three coming up." He waited until the van was out of sight and then started the car and eased from the curb, careful to keep well back.

"I got the address of the house," Annie said as they drove slowly past. She dug in her handbag for a notepad and jotted it down. "I'll bet that house is fully furnished with boosted goods."

"Call Chris," Jake said.

"Good idea." Annie got out her cell, called Cranston's, and was put through to Chris immediately. She filled him in on their progress. "You can probably move those TVs away from the front of the store now. No use attracting any more flies."

Chris laughed and Annie promised to keep him informed.

Annie had propped Jake's cell phone on the dash and Jake kept his eye on the red dot. "It's moving fast now," he said.

"He's on the freeway. I hope he's not leaving town."

"Doesn't matter. The tracker uses cell towers. We can find him anywhere."

"He's pulling off again," Annie said. "Step it up a bit."

Jake followed the route the van took and, in five minutes, pulled off the freeway into an industrial area. The red dot indicated the van had stopped two blocks away.

"Should we drive by?" Jake asked.

"Better idea. Stop back half a block and we'll walk up and see what's going on."

Jake pulled the Firebird over a hundred feet short of the suspected industrial unit and they got out, walked up the sidewalk, and approached the building.

"He's likely behind the unit," Jake said. "They'll be unloading through a back door."

Annie started ahead, moving toward the side of the building. "I want to make sure this is the right place before we call the police."

Jake followed her along the side of the unit to the back of the building. "This is it," he whispered, glancing around the corner. The van was backed up to an overhead door, and men unloaded the goods, carrying everything inside.

"We got them," Annie said, dialing Hank's number.

Hank and Jake had been fast friends since high school, sharing a love of football and good times. When Jake and Annie had met, the three became almost inseparable. Their friendship had grown tighter over the years and, at a time like this, the detective was the one to call.

When the cop answered, she gave him a quick version of the story along with the address of the building as they hustled back toward the street.

"Wow. Good job, guys, but I can't come now. King and I are about to execute a search warrant. I'll talk to dispatch and we'll get some cars there immediately."

Annie hung up. "We've done our part. We might as well wait." They crossed the street and sat under a tree. In a few minutes, a black van pulled up silently and spun into the lot, and an elite team dressed in full SWAT gear poured out and surrounded the building.

The Lincolns crossed the street, staying behind the team as they moved to the rear of the unit. Through the large overhead door they saw row after row of items, sorted and stacked on shelves.

Half a dozen men were cuffed and loaded into a paddy wagon that had followed the team in.

Jake put his arm around Annie as they watched the arrests. "Those guys will be going away for a while. Congratulations, my dear."

Annie smiled up at Jake. "Thanks, but you helped a little bit."

CHAPTER 10

Tuesday, 10:49 a.m.

HANK WAS ABLE TO obtain a warrant for the search of Michael Norton's residence, and after contacting Sterling Auto Parts, where Norton worked as a production line operator, Hank was informed he hadn't clocked in to work that day. According to Sterling's records, Norton had left the day before at 5:00 pm. That's all they could tell him of the whereabouts of Michael Norton.

There was no other option but to try Norton's house in case he'd taken the day off, as well as execute the search warrant they had secured.

According to the information Hank had, Norton lived with his wife, Tammy, in an older part of the city. Hank followed a pair of cruisers down the narrow street. Mature maple trees lined both sides, their branches overhanging.

The cruisers pulled in front of the Norton house, a small, weather-beaten bungalow sorely in need of roof repairs. The peeling clapboard exterior could do with a fresh coat of paint, and the one-time flower bed had turned to a nest of weeds and wild grass.

Hank parked behind the cruisers, and the detectives followed two officers past the dark blue 1996 Ford Probe parked in the driveway. They took the crumbling concrete pathway to the front door. Two other officers cut around beside the building to the backyard. They would guard against any attempt at escape.

Hank rang the doorbell and waited patiently. The door was opened a moment later by a woman clad in a tattered white housecoat. She brushed back her disheveled midlength hair with one hand, holding her housecoat tightly around her throat with the other.

She looked at Hank, then at the officers behind him, and frowned. "Yes?"

Hank held up the warrant. "I have a search warrant for these premises. We'd also very much like to speak to Michael Norton."

Her frown deepened. "He … he's not here." Her eyes darted back and forth between the two detectives. "What's going on?"

Hank pushed gently at the door. "Please open the door, ma'am."

She stepped back, wrapped her arms around herself, and watched them fearfully.

Hank motioned toward the officers, their hands on their weapons. "Search the house."

The officers and King moved forward and, room by

room, the house was searched. Michael Norton was not home.

Tammy Norton had moved into the living room and stood by a small brick fireplace. Hank joined her. "Do you know where your husband is?" he asked.

Mrs. Norton shook her head. "He didn't come home last night. He went to work in the morning and that's the last I saw of him." She paused. "What's this all about? What's he done?"

"Do you know where he might be?"

Lines of worry showed on Tammy Norton's face. "I ... I don't know. Can't you tell me what's going on?"

"He's wanted for questioning in a murder case, ma'am."

Mrs. Norton's mouth dropped open and she sank into a chair and leaned forward. "Murder?" She rested her head in her hands and sat still a moment. Finally, she looked up, confusion and pleading on her face. "There must be some mistake?"

"What is your, or your husband's, relationship with Werner Shaft?" Hank asked.

She sat back and frowned. "I hardly know him. He and my husband were in prison together a few years ago, and as far as I know, they haven't seen each other since."

Hank sat on the edge of the couch and pulled out his notepad and pen. "Do either you or your husband own a gun?"

"No, I sure don't. And I don't think my husband does anymore. After his time in prison, he settled down and works hard. He hasn't been in any kind of trouble since." She tilted her head slightly. "Are you sure you have the right man?"

Hank disregarded her question and looked at his notes. "Does your husband drive a white Honda Accord?"

She nodded.

King came into the room. "There's no car in the garage." He looked at Mrs. Norton. "Does your husband own a plaid shirt?"

She looked at King. "Yes, he's fond of plaid. He owns several."

"The closet is full of them," King said to Hank. "According to the witness, the killer wore a plaid shirt."

"A lot of people own plaid shirts," Hank said. He made a note in his pad.

King held up a small green plastic box placed inside an evidence bag. "I found this in the basement. A box of thirty-eight-caliber cartridges. It's empty."

Hank looked at the box. "No weapon?"

"Can't find a gun anywhere."

"Not surprising. If he didn't come home, he still has it with him."

Mrs. Norton's eyes moved back and forth between the box and the two detectives, her face clouded with confusion.

"Keep looking," Hank said to King, and then turned back to Mrs. Norton. "Do you have any idea where your husband might be?"

She shook her head. "He always comes home after work. I can't understand it. Something must've happened to him."

"King," Hank called. He went out to the hallway, where the detective stopped and turned around. "Get a BOLO out on Norton right away. And also on his car. If this guy's on the run, he might be using his own vehicle."

"Done."

Hank went back to the front room and sat on the couch.

"Detective," Mrs. Norton said. "Michael has some family in Toronto. Perhaps he went there."

"We'll check," Hank said. "I'll need their names and addresses as well as a list of all his acquaintances."

"I can do that right away. I hope you find him and he can clear this up." She fidgeted with her hands as she spoke. "My husband didn't murder anyone. I'm sure of that."

"The sooner we find him, the quicker we can sort this out, Mrs. Norton. Whatever you can do to help will make things go faster."

She leaned forward and looked intently at Hank. "I'll help any way I can. I'm worried about my husband. He might be in danger."

Hank stood. "We'll do our best to find him. Thank you, Mrs. Norton." He tucked his notepad away and turned to leave. "An officer will stay here until you have the list ready."

Hank found King looking through the kitchen cupboards. "Anything interesting?" Hank asked.

"Nothing." King closed the cupboard door and turned to Hank. "I guess we're done here for now."

Hank instructed an officer to stay and wait for the list. On the way out he gave Mrs. Norton his card and asked her to contact him if she heard from her husband. He and King left the house, went to the car, and got in.

King turned to Hank. "Any more leads to follow?"

Hank leaned back in his seat and let out a long breath. "Not right now. As soon as Mrs. Norton gets that list together, I want you to check them out. Norton's hiding somewhere."

"Anything else?"

"I'm going to visit Richmond Distributing to talk to Werner Shaft's coworkers. One of them might know something." He started the car and pulled away from the curb. "And then we'll wait for the forensic report and the ME's report and see if they have anything for us."

As they drove back to the precinct, they discussed what little they knew of the case. Hank was hard-pressed to come up with a motive, and until they found Michael Norton, there was little else they could do.

CHAPTER 11

Tuesday, 11:39 a.m.

ANNIE CALLED CHRIS and updated him on the arrest of the members of the organization plaguing Cranston's. The head of security was amazed at the complexity and extent of the operation that had targeted the store.

Cranston's was not the only retailer hit so hard. The group of thieves had earmarked grocery stores and pharmacies as well, and their inventory of items covered almost every aspect of retail goods imaginable.

Annie was making detailed notes outlining the successful operation when the phone on her desk rang.

The caller introduced herself as Maria Shaft. "Mrs. Lincoln," the woman said and sighed deeply. "My husband was murdered yesterday, and although the police have a suspect, it seems he's fled."

"I'm sorry to hear about your husband, Mrs. Shaft. Please call me Annie. What can we do to help?"

"I want you to find my husband's killer."

Annie hesitated. "The police are capable of handling this. They have a lot more resources at their disposal than we do."

"Nonetheless, I'd like you to help, if you're willing." Her voice broke and she paused a moment. "My husband was a good man and I want his killer found and stopped."

Annie asked the woman to hold and went to the kitchen, where Jake sat at the table, reading the newspaper. She explained the phone call and the caller's request.

"We have nothing pressing right now," Jake said. "It won't hurt to talk to her."

"What can we do that the police can't?" Annie asked.

Jake shrugged. "Who knows?"

Annie realized, as the head of RHPD robbery/homicide, Hank would be responsible for this case. He was as capable as any detective, and better than most. Nonetheless, they could look into it.

"We'll go and see her," Annie said and went back to the office. She made arrangements with Mrs. Shaft to visit her right away.

She hung up the phone thoughtfully. If they chose to take the case, she knew Hank would be willing to share any information he had with them. He often said they were on the same side, so why keep secrets? Justice was more important to him than territory.

Although some cops in the precinct objected to their close relationship with the homicide detective, Captain Diego didn't argue all that strenuously. Their success was his success, and gave him another notch in his belt. The captain had recently gone so far as to offer them positions as auxiliary constables—which they had politely declined.

It didn't take Jake long to get ready. He picked his keys from a wicker basket in the kitchen, tucked his cell phone in its holder, and stood by the front door, waiting for her.

Annie shut down her computer, changed her clothes, and grabbed her handbag containing a notepad, a digital recorder, and her cell phone, along with a variety of other necessities.

Jake had tired of waiting and pulled the Firebird from the garage, revving it up when she got in.

A few minutes later they parked in front of Maria Shaft's residence, went up the walkway, and rang the bell.

Mrs. Shaft opened the door, they introduced themselves, and she ushered them in.

A man stood by a brick fireplace at the far side of the living room. He turned when they entered, approached them, and held out a hand. "Rocky Shaft. Werner's brother."

The man looked to be midthirties, casually dressed, with a long, solemn face as grim and unsmiling as Maria's. They both appeared to be under a lot of strain, understandable given the circumstances.

They shook his offered hand and he waved toward the couch. Mrs. Shaft sat in an armchair while Rocky stood by her side, one hand on the back of her chair, a perpetual frown on his face.

Maria Shaft spoke first. "I talked to Detective Hank Corning earlier. He's been helpful in answering our questions, but I feel with your help there might be a better chance of finding Michael Norton before he disappears forever."

Jake smiled. "We don't know Michael Norton or anything at all about this. Maybe we should start at the beginning, Mrs. Shaft."

"I'm sorry. Of course." Mrs. Shaft offered a faint smile, leaned forward, and clasped her hands in her lap. "Michael Norton is the suspect in my husband's murder, but he's nowhere to be found." She paused. "Please call me Maria."

Annie removed the digital recorder from her bag, switched it on, and set it on the coffee table between them. "I hope you don't mind if I record this?"

"I don't mind at all."

"Please tell us everything you know, Maria," Annie said.

Maria Shaft stopped often to wipe a tear or stifle a sob as she explained how the murder was believed to have taken place and exactly who the suspect was.

Rocky stood, unmoving all the while. When she finished, he crossed his arms and said, "I know this Norton character. He's bad news. My brother finally got his life straightened out and things were going good for him." He looked down at Maria. "Weren't they, Maria?"

She nodded and wiped a tear. "He was a good husband."

"What about a motive?" Annie asked. "What reason would Norton have to kill Werner?"

"I've been thinking about that," Rocky said. "Perhaps Norton is involved in something criminal again. Maybe he approached Werner about helping him, and Werner threatened to turn him in."

"But weren't they friends?" Jake asked.

Rocky shook his head emphatically. "After prison, they went their separate ways. As far as I know, they haven't seen each other for a long time. But I could be wrong."

"Are you convinced Michael Norton is the killer?" Jake asked.

"The police have evidence against him, and, given his history, I believe so."

"But why would he run?"

"Perhaps he was afraid the witness saw his face," Annie suggested.

Jake looked at Annie. "Could be that. Or maybe there's something else Norton's afraid will come to light."

Annie picked up her recorder, shut it off, and dropped it into her handbag. "We'll have to work on some ideas and see what we come up with." She stood. "We'll do some preliminary investigation and let you know."

Jake stood. "Don't give up on the police yet. Hank Corning is a friend of ours, and he's a good cop." He looked at Annie, then back at Maria. "Between us and Detective Corning, we should be able to track this guy down."

Maria rose and smiled. "Thank you. I can't bear the thought of that man going free after what he did."

They shook hands and Rocky escorted them to the door. "Don't worry about payment," he said. "Werner had some savings and I'm willing to kick in. Just find my brother's killer."

"We'll do all we can and let you know," Jake said as he and Annie stepped outside.

They got in the car, and as they drove away, Annie said, "I'm still not so sure about this case. Hank's quite capable."

Jake looked at her and shrugged. "I'm willing to stick at it unless something else pops up."

Annie nodded. "Let me go over my notes and I'll let you know what I think."

CHAPTER 12

Tuesday, 12:18 p.m.

HANK HAD DROPPED in to Richmond Distributing and talked to everyone there who worked with, or knew, Werner Shaft. Most of them had displayed shock when they learned of his murder. It seemed Shaft was well liked, a reasonably good warehouse manager, and nobody could think of anything unusual or suspicious happening that day, or any other day, involving him.

The story he pieced together was that Shaft had come into work on Monday and clocked out as usual at 7:00 p.m., and he hadn't been heard from since.

Werner's brother, Rocky, was at work that day as well, and the story was much the same—business as usual. He was there until 7:00 p.m. on Monday, and Tuesday morning he clocked in but left shortly thereafter, presumably when Maria called him regarding the murder of his brother. Hank hadn't interviewed Rocky—that would be forthcoming.

King had obtained the list of Michael Norton's family and friends from Norton's wife, Tammy, and he would be doing a series of interviews. He'd likely be gone most of the day. Hank didn't hold out much hope for results at that end. It seemed unlikely Norton would kill somebody, then hide out at one of the most obvious places.

When Hank got back to the precinct, he was pleased to see the ME's report regarding the murder of Werner Shaft waiting on his desk. He picked up the folder, and underneath it were the forensic and ballistics reports. Jameson had kept his word and processed the evidence in record time.

He leafed through the ME's report, slipped the summary page from the stack of papers, and browsed it. Her findings on Werner Shaft weren't a surprise. The observations Hank made at the crime scene proved to be correct.

Report of Findings on the Death of Werner Shaft

Cause of death: gunshot wound to the head.
Manner of death: homicide.
Blood alcohol: negative.
Blood drug screens: negative.
Urine drug screens: negative.

My examination of the body of Werner Shaft revealed a gunshot wound to the head, with the entrance wound on the forehead, and the exit wound on the rear of the head. The trajectory of the bullet that went through Werner Shaft's head was front to back, fired from a distance of eighteen to twenty-four inches.

Werner Shaft also received a gunshot wound to the back, entering approximately one inch from the center. The trajectory of the bullet was through the spinal cord, lodging in the heart. The lack of gunshot residue indicates the shot came from a distance of five feet or greater.

Werner Shaft also received a nonfatal gunshot wound to the left shoulder, two inches down from the top surface of the shoulder, entering the deltoid muscle from the rear at approximately a forty-five-degree angle. The bullet exited the front of the body. The lack of gunshot residue, along with the angle of penetration, indicates the shot came from a distance of five feet or greater.

In my opinion, Werner Shaft died of a gunshot wound to the head. Manner of death is homicide.

The ballistics report was much more interesting and enlightening.

Two shell casings had been found in the lane beside Master Footwear, one more at the rear. All three came from Shaft's weapon. In the alleyway between the two buildings, two more casings had been found, one at the entranceway to the alley, one close by the body. Both were from an unknown weapon.

Except for the bullet found in Shaft's heart and the one that had embedded itself in the ground under his head, the rest of them had not been found, having missed their target.

That all fit in perfectly with the statement of the witness.

The forensic report stated that the empty cartridge box found in Norton's basement had his fingerprints on it. That wasn't surprising. It was Norton's house.

What made Hank sit forward was the discovery of a partial fingerprint on the casing found beside the body. That fingerprint was identified as belonging to Michael Norton.

Now he had enough for an arrest warrant. All he needed to do was find Norton.

He leaned back, trying to decide what his next move was. He was waiting to see if King uncovered anything, hoping Norton or his car would be found, and praying for a solid lead.

His ringing cell phone brought him out of his thoughts. It was Jake.

"Afternoon, Hank," Jake said when the detective answered the phone.

Hank tilted his chair back and rested his foot on an open desk drawer. "Congratulations to both of you for the sting you set up. I hear they brought in a lot of guys. Wish I could've been there."

Jake chuckled. "Maybe next time, Hank. You can't be everywhere at once."

"Diego is pretty happy. I understand Cranston's is over the moon about it. King is the only one who didn't have anything good to say. No surprise there."

"What about the low-level guys? The boosters?" Jake asked.

Hank laughed. "I'm pretty sure we'll find somebody who'll talk and we'll nab some of them. The rest'll be out of business anyway, with no place to sell the stuff."

"Another bunch will spring up," Jake said. "I don't think there'll ever be an end to organized shoplifting."

"Afraid you're right."

Jake cleared his throat. "Hank, do you know somebody by the name of Maria Shaft?"

Hank sat forward. "I sure do. Where'd you get that name?"

"She called us. I assumed this would be your case. She wants us to find her husband's killer."

"She's in a mighty hurry, isn't she? I only told her about her husband's murder this morning."

"She heard the suspect, Michael Norton, ran," Jake said. "She wants us to track him down before he disappears."

"She's already called me twice since this morning," Hank said. "She doesn't understand these things can take some time. I filled her in on what we know so far, but there's not much to go on. Right now we're trying to find Norton. Been talking to most everyone he knows. So far, no luck."

"We don't want to step on your toes, Hank. We didn't tell Maria Shaft we'd take the case for sure. We said we'd look into it."

"It doesn't matter to me. You guys are welcome to everything I have. You know how I feel about that."

"Appreciate it, Hank."

"I'll get together a package and get it to you. Right now, I'm running out of leads, so I might have time to drop by there later today."

"Look forward to it," Jake said and they hung up.

Hank picked up his briefcase, dropped the reports inside, and pushed back his chair.

According to his latest conversation with Mrs. Shaft, her brother-in-law was there with her today. He would pay Rocky Shaft a visit, wrapping up his entire list of leads and possible suspects.

CHAPTER 13

Tuesday, 12:43 p.m.

LISA KRUNK was a legend in her own mind. With eyes and ears everywhere, there wasn't much in this dumpy little town that passed her by. Her many years as a television journalist, and her dogged determination, ensured that.

The evening before, when she'd gotten wind of the murder of Werner Shaft, she leaped into action. If she hadn't been chasing some dead-end story on the other side of the city, she would've made it to the crime scene before the body was taken away.

As it was, her trusty cameraman, Don, got a few shots of cops hanging around, the flashy yellow tape everywhere, and the ambulance pulling away with its load. She was able to corner a couple of cops who knew next to nothing about what happened. The whole thing was a big disappointment.

Via her sources, she pieced together most of the facts of what had gone on, and now, those same sources confirmed the police had a suspect. His name was Michael Norton. A few minutes of research netted her the relationship between Shaft and Norton.

She also obtained the name of the victim's wife, Mrs. Maria Shaft. And that's where she had to start her story.

Don pulled the Channel 7 Action News van to the curb in front of the Shaft residence. Lisa hopped from the passenger-side door while Don grabbed the camera equipment from the back and hurried to catch up.

"Don, roll the camera now. We don't want to miss anything."

Don dropped the camera on his shoulder, and in a moment the red light glowed. He aimed it toward the house and hurried up the walkway behind Lisa.

She rang the bell and stood back. There was no answer. She glanced toward the driveway. A dark green Mazda was parked in front of the garage. Someone must be home.

She rang the bell again. Finally, the door opened a crack and a woman stuck her nose out.

"Maria Shaft?" Lisa asked.

The woman nodded. "Yes?"

"I'm Lisa Krunk from Channel 7 Action News. Could I ask you a few questions regarding the murder of your husband?"

The woman frowned, and then the frown disappeared as her lips curled into a weak smile. "Yes," she said and opened the door, motioning for them to enter.

Lisa stepped inside the foyer, Don close behind, and they followed her into the front room.

Maria sat, Don stood, and Lisa moved in.

"Mrs. Shaft," Lisa said, the microphone on and poised. "I'm sorry to hear about the murder of your husband." She continued with her pretense of sympathy. "Our thoughts and prayers are with you at this time and I'm sure my viewers will express the same concern."

The words almost made her gag, but she spewed them out, realizing it was the best way to get on the interviewee's good side before moving in for the kill—so to speak.

Maria Shaft smiled weakly. "Thank you."

Lisa pulled a footstool in close, sat down, and leaned in. "Tell me about your husband, Mrs. Shaft," she said, pushing the microphone at the woman.

Maria glanced at the mike, closed her eyes, and took a deep breath. She opened her eyes again and spoke. "My husband was a good man and didn't deserve this." She looked at the camera trained on her face. "I want everyone to know that."

Lisa spoke again, "Mrs. Shaft." She paused. "May I call you Maria?"

Maria Shaft nodded.

Lisa continued, "Maria, what can you tell me about the relationship between your husband and the suspect, Michael Norton?"

Maria's face darkened. "There's no relationship and there hasn't been for years."

Time to move in with the heavy artillery. "Maria, I understand your husband and Norton were convicted of burglary several years ago. Would you not call that a relationship?"

Maria scowled. "That was a long time ago, in another lifetime. A lot has happened since then."

Lisa nodded encouragingly and forced a sympathetic smile to cross her wide mouth. "After all this time, why do you think Michael Norton would kill your husband? Was it for revenge?"

Maria looked at the camera again, her eyes moistening. "I don't know. The police are doing what they can, and I've retained a private investigation firm to help. If anyone out there knows anything, please let me know."

Lisa stood, hugged the mike, and looked down her long, sharp nose at the camera. "I urge my viewers to contact me directly if they have any information as to the whereabouts of this man." She paused. She would edit in a photo of Norton at this point.

She sat back down and faced Maria again. The woman was looking toward the door. Lisa followed her gaze to a man standing inside the doorway, a heavy frown on his face.

"What's this all about?" he asked, looking at Lisa.

Lisa stood and approached him, thinking quickly, the eye of the camera following. "I'm doing a story on the tragic murder of Werner Shaft, and I wanted to give Maria a chance to air her thoughts."

"Maria has been under enough strain lately," he said, glancing at the woman in the chair who dabbed gently at her eyes with a tissue.

"It's all right, Rocky," Maria said. "If they can help track down Michael Norton, it's a good thing."

Rocky's jaw clenched and he moved in closer to Maria, his

eyes on Lisa. "We want that killer caught." He cursed, faced the camera, and pummeled the suspect with his words. His language become more offensive as his anger increased.

Lisa didn't mind. She could bleep out those words, viewers would fill in the blanks, and the effect would be the same. Maybe even better.

Rocky glared at the red light and leaned in, his face flushed. He clenched his fists. "If I get ahold of you, I'll break your worthless neck. You killed my brother, you son of—"

Maria interrupted him with a hand on his arm, her eyes pleading. "Rocky, calm down."

Rocky took a deep breath and moved back a step. "Sorry. I'm upset, that's all."

Lisa smiled outwardly, smothering an inner jump for joy. "That's okay," she said in her calmest voice. "It's understandable." What she really wanted was more of the same. It was good stuff, and would keep her viewers glued to their screens.

Maria looked up at Rocky. "I know you wouldn't kill the man. We'll let the law take care of him."

Rocky looked at Maria, his eyes flaring, and stormed from the room. The camera followed his retreat and then turned back to Maria.

The grieving widow gave a lopsided smile. "Please forgive Rocky. He's stressed out." She added quickly, "We both are."

"It's all right, Maria," Lisa said. "Let's hope, with the help of our viewers, we can bring your husband's killer to justice."

Maria dabbed at a tear rolling down her cheek, then balled up the tissue in her tightly clenched hands. She looked at Lisa and spoke firmly. "Perhaps we'd better end this interview."

Lisa understood the woman's tone of voice and knew she wouldn't get anything else of use. She smiled politely, thanked Maria for her time, and wished her well.

Don shut down the camera and followed her back to the van. Lisa was pleased with the interview. Perhaps she would get it edited as soon as possible, run a short version every hour, and then edit in footage from the crime scene, do some interesting voice-overs, and dump the whole thing on the public at six o'clock.

CHAPTER 14

Tuesday, 1:05 p.m.

ANNIE CLEANED UP THE lunch dishes, made herself a cup of coffee, and went into the office. She had discussed the case with Jake earlier, and they had decided to do what they could to help Maria Shaft. After calling Maria, Jake had picked up a retainer, and Annie was ready to delve into the case.

She sat at her desk and booted up her computer. Hank was on his way over and she planned to kill time by doing some preliminary research on Werner Shaft and Michael Norton.

A quick search under both names brought up a story on their relationship nine years ago. They were convicted of breaking into a warehouse and stealing a quantity of electronic equipment. They got nabbed when the fence they contacted turned out to be an undercover cop. Each had pled guilty and done a three-year stint in prison.

The first few links in the search led to a variety of news sources featuring the same information with minor variations.

Then an item caught her eye on the second page of the search results. She clicked through and was presented with a story from less than a year ago.

She read the headline: *Werner Shaft Wins 5th Annual Smokie's Bar 9-Ball Tournament.*

There was a picture identifying the subject as Werner Shaft as he stood by a billiard table, proudly holding a trophy in one hand, his cue in the other.

What made her sit forward was the story below the picture identifying the runner-up as Michael Norton. There was no photo of Norton, but there was little doubt; it had to be the same man.

The next item on the search revealed that a small local cable TV company had done a short video interview with Shaft and Norton following the tournament. It was featured on their neighborhood news segment. Annie watched the brief interview with interest.

It wasn't evidence of any criminal activity, but Rocky Shaft had said there was no relationship between his brother and the fugitive, Michael Norton. And Maria had agreed. Yet there clearly was.

Rocky was mistaken—nothing suspicious in that, but this was evidence the two ex-cons had kept in some kind of contact since their time in prison.

Annie wondered why Maria Shaft wasn't aware of it. Surely Werner would've boasted about his tournament win to her. But perhaps not, and either way, it didn't prove much.

She downloaded the interview video, and then printed out the news story and tucked it inside the thin file she had started on the case. Her search yielded nothing else of interest, so she closed the folder, brought it to the living room, and dropped it on the coffee table. She would show it to Hank and see what he thought about it.

She had just curled up with a book when the doorbell rang. Jake came down from upstairs and beat her to the door, and in a moment Hank and Jake came into the room and sat on the couch.

Hank greeted her, set his briefcase on the cushion between him and Jake, and snapped it open. He pulled out two folders, handing one to Jake, the other to Annie.

"That's all we have right now and you're welcome to it," Hank said. "There's the ME's report on the murder, the forensic report, the witness statement, and whatever else we could dig up."

"There's one more thing," Annie said. "It appears Shaft and Norton did have a relationship after all." She told him about the news story she'd found online regarding the nine-ball tournament, handing him the printout.

He read it and said, "I talked to Tammy Norton and she told me there was no relationship between Shaft and Norton. Said they hadn't seen each other for years. Both wives claim they knew nothing about their association." Hank waved the printout. "But this tells me the two men had something going on."

"Something they wanted to keep secret," Jake added. "Didn't want their wives to know."

"Exactly. I don't think Tammy would have any reason to lie about it," Hank said. "If she knew about their association, she would've said something. She wants to find her husband as badly as we do and she seems sure he's innocent."

"Wives are always the last to know," Annie said.

Jake was perusing the forensics report. He dropped it in his lap and looked at Hank. "This sure doesn't look like a professional hit. A professional would've been more efficient than this."

"A bullet in the head is pretty efficient," Annie said.

"I mean the way it was carried out. A chase and a lot of shots. A hitman would've done it in one. Game over."

"Exactly," Hank said. "And he wouldn't have done it where there could be witnesses."

Jake added, "A pro would never have left shell casings laying around either. Especially ones with his fingerprints on them."

Annie sat forward, her brow wrinkled in thought. "If Werner Shaft wasn't involved in anything criminal since being released from prison, then why was he carrying a gun?"

"Perhaps he knew his life was in danger. Maybe he was threatened and carried it for protection."

"Or perhaps," Hank said, "he was still involved in something his wife didn't know about."

"Both wives said the same thing," Jake said. "Their husbands had gone straight. So if they were up to no good and working together, they kept it to themselves."

"I'm still lacking a motive," Hank said.

"Love or money," Jake said. "It's always about love or money."

Annie looked at Hank. "Is there evidence of any affairs going on anywhere?"

"We're looking into that," Hank said.

"What about between Rocky Shaft and Maria?" Jake asked. "Could Rocky Shaft have killed his own brother because he's having an affair with his brother's wife? He lives with them and has the opportunity."

"It's a possibility," Hank said. "That's something we're looking into, but it might be a hard thing to prove. And right now, King is interviewing Michael Norton's list of family and friends. His objective is to dig up the whereabouts of Norton, but I'm sure he'll be asking a lot of pointed questions while he's at it."

Hank continued, "I dropped by Michael Norton's workplace on the way here. He's never missed a day in recent history. He was there on Monday and clocked out as usual."

"And his coworkers?" Jake asked.

"None of them could shed any light on this. He never had a run-in with anyone, and nothing seemed suspicious or out of place as far as they could tell."

Jake waved the file folder. "You don't have anything in here on Rocky Shaft."

"He wasn't there when I first went to see Mrs. Shaft. I dropped in again a few minutes ago and Rocky was there this time, but there's no report yet."

"What did you think of Rocky?" Annie asked.

"He's a very angry man," Hank said. "But that's understandable, given the circumstances."

"Did he have anything else to say?"

"Nothing new to add," Hank said. "He basically repeated what I've heard before. But there was one interesting occurrence."

"Regarding Rocky?" Annie asked.

"Regarding Lisa Krunk," Hank said. "According to Maria, Lisa dropped by, and she and Rocky ended up succumbing to one of her interviews."

Annie frowned. "Lisa's interviews never go well. She always finds some way to make everyone look bad."

"I wish they'd kept away from Lisa," Hank said. "But Maria has a right to know how we're proceeding, and she has a right to talk to the news people. There's nothing we can do about that. And it's important to get Norton's picture out there. Right now, our goal is to track him down. There's not much else we can do until that happens."

"If you have no objections, Hank," Annie said, "I'd like to pay Tammy Norton a visit this afternoon."

"I have no objections," Hank said.

CHAPTER 15

Tuesday, 1:38 p.m.

JAKE WAITED IN the office while Annie made a call to Tammy Norton. The woman said she would be home all afternoon and was eager to help in the investigation.

"I'd like to go now if you have nothing else to do," Annie said to Jake after she hung up the phone.

"My schedule is open," Jake said.

"Do you even have a schedule?"

"I keep it in my head. That way it never gets misplaced."

Annie pushed back her chair and stood. "I'll meet you outside, then."

Jake grabbed his keys and pulled the Firebird from the garage. A minute later, Annie joined him and they roared from the driveway.

When they pulled up to the curb in front of the Norton residence a few minutes later, Jake glanced at the crumbling house. "What does this guy do for a living?"

"He's a production line worker," Annie said as she opened her door and stepped out. "Meaning, he works on an assembly line."

Jake got out of the car, glanced at the dark blue Ford Probe in the driveway, and followed Annie up the pathway to the front door. She rang the bell.

Tammy Norton answered the door, a forced smile on her face. "Are you the Lincolns?"

"We are," Annie said, and Tammy led them into the front room and motioned toward the couch while she sat in an armchair.

They sat down and Annie spoke first. "Mrs. Norton, I want to tell you up front, we've been retained by Maria Shaft to find your husband."

"Please, call me Tammy, and I'm aware he's a suspect. I'm sure he's not guilty, and I'm as eager to find him as the police are. I'm so afraid something has happened to him." Her smile was replaced with a worried frown.

"We realize you've already spoken to Detective Corning," Jake said. "But we have a few questions for you."

Tammy nodded, brushed back a strand of dark hair, and leaned forward.

Annie pulled a file folder from her large handbag and laid it in her lap. She smiled. "Tammy, Maria Shaft indicated her husband and yours haven't associated since being released from prison, and you said the same to Detective Corning." She opened the file folder, slipped out the printout of the nine-ball tournament, and handed it to Tammy. "Were you aware of this?"

Tammy took the paper and browsed it. Her frown deepened. "I knew Michael played nine-ball at the pub on occasion." She waved the paper. "But I wasn't aware Werner Shaft was part of it."

"For some reason," Jake said, "both of them wanted to keep it from their wives."

"But why?" Tammy asked, handing back the paper.

"We think they were involved in something together," Annie said. "Something illegal."

Tammy's frown took over her whole face, revealing a hint of indignation. "That's absurd."

"Perhaps," Annie said. "But Werner Shaft was murdered for some reason."

Tammy reached on the stand beside her and pulled a tissue from a box. She wiped at some tears and took a deep breath. "Find my husband and this will all be cleared up."

"We need your help with that," Jake said. "So far, he has eluded the police."

Tammy sobbed and wiped her face again. She shook her head slowly. "I don't know where he is."

Jake tilted his head and looked sideways at Annie. She was leaned forward, squinting at Tammy. She stood and moved closer to the woman, bending over. Tammy looked back, confusion on her face.

"Tammy, how did you get those marks on your face?"

The woman's hand shot up, covering the side of her left eye.

Annie reached out and gently grasped Tammy's wrist and tugged her hand away.

Jake leaned forward and peered closer. He could see a bruise by her left eye. It looked like she had tried to cover it with makeup and wiped the covering away along with her tears.

"I ... hurt myself. I ... slipped on the stairs and took a tumble."

Tammy sat silently as Annie put her hand under the woman's chin, tilting her head back. Annie rubbed at a spot, revealing another attempt at hiding a bruise.

Annie sat back down. "Tammy, did your husband do that?"

Tammy's face took on a look of anger, and then it softened and she dropped her head. She sobbed and wiped away another tear, now making no attempt to hide the marks on her face.

"Tell me, Tammy. It's important," Annie said.

The woman kept her head bowed and nodded weakly.

"Does he beat you up?"

She shrugged one shoulder.

Annie stood and approached the woman again. She leaned down, put a hand under Tammy's chin, and tilted her head up. "Tell me," Annie said in a soft voice.

Tammy looked Annie in the eye and nodded. "Sometimes," she said. "But I was ashamed to say anything about it."

"Why are you defending him?" Jake asked.

Tammy's nostrils flared and her face reddened. "Because he's my husband."

"Is that why you're willing to help us?" Jake asked. "Because you're afraid of him?"

84

Tammy took a deep breath and closed her eyes. When she opened them again, she said, "Yes, I'm afraid of him. He ... he's changed lately." She narrowed her eyes. "He never used to be like this, but now ..."

Annie waved the printout. "Did you know about their relationship?"

Tammy shook her head. "I honestly didn't."

"But you think he's guilty of murder, don't you?"

The woman's shoulders slumped and she sighed. "No."

"Other than yourself," Jake asked, "has he been violent toward others?"

"Not that I know of." She paused. "He can get angry easily, but I've never seen him get into an altercation with anyone."

"Just with you?"

Tammy shrugged again. "I seem to irritate him somehow."

"It's not your fault," Jake said gently. "And it's nothing to be ashamed of."

Annie was browsing the police reports. She looked up. "Were you aware he owned a gun?"

The woman shook her head adamantly. "The police said they found ammunition in the basement somewhere. I don't go down there often."

"And his fingerprint was found on a shell casing at the murder scene," Annie said.

Tammy's eyes bulged. "I don't believe it. He might've hit me from time to time, but he would never kill anyone."

"And a witness saw his car there."

Tammy was silent.

"Now do you believe it?" Jake asked.

Tammy closed her eyes and took a few quick breaths. "No, I don't believe it," she said.

"How can we find him and prove he didn't do it?" Annie asked.

"I don't know," the woman said. "I honestly don't know."

Annie put the printout back into the folder, tucked it into her handbag, then looked at Jake and stood.

Jake pulled a business card from his shirt pocket and handed it to Tammy. "Call us if you think of something that can help us find your husband. Or you can call the police."

Tammy took the card, stood, and followed them quietly to the door. "Let me know if you find anything," she said.

Annie promised her they would, then followed Jake to the car and got in.

"After all that," Jake said, turning to Annie, "she still defends him."

Annie sighed. "They almost always do."

CHAPTER 16

Tuesday, 2:54 p.m.

THE MAN WAITED patiently, glancing at his watch more than once, spinning the cylinder on his revolver often, humming a nameless tune all the while.

His quarry wasn't at home and time was wasting, but he was being well paid for this job, so wait he would. As long as it took. He prided himself on getting the job done perfectly every time. And this time would be no different.

From where he sat in the comfortable living room, he could see the driveway and half the street. He would know when they arrived, and would have time to prepare for the ambush that would earn him his pay.

He looked at his watch again. He knew they had a kid, and if he got home from school before the job was finished, that could complicate things somewhat. However, he had no qualms about taking out the boy as well, if necessary. It would be the first time he ever killed a kid, but you had to start sometime.

He smiled grimly as a car roared into the driveway. It was a big, shiny red Firebird. They were here. He slid from the chair, circled into the kitchen, and waited. He decided the best plan of action would be to sit tight until they were inside, then step into the hallway and nail them both at once before they could react.

He knew how important the element of surprise was.

Then the car roared once more and he frowned. It sounded like they were leaving again. He circled back into the living room and eased to the front window in time to see the Firebird turn from the driveway and head up the street.

Now what?

And then a key rattled in the door and he froze. It must be the woman. The guy had probably dropped her off and left again.

He didn't have time to get back to the kitchen. He would have to wait until she came in, then go into the hallway and take her out from behind. He didn't often shoot people in the back. He preferred to see their faces as they went down, but he would have to make an exception this time. It was either that or risk failing—something he never did.

He ducked behind the chair and peered around. He could barely see into the hallway at the front of the house. He heard the door open and someone step in, and then the sound of the door snapping closed.

It was a woman. He heard her singing softly. Some stupid '80s song.

He was faced with a minor dilemma. He could kill the woman first, wait for the man to return, and then nail him the same way. The problem was, someone might hear the gunfire, and he didn't like to hang around for long after the first shot was fired. That could get him caught.

He had wanted to get both at once. It was always easier that way. Taking out only one would put the other on his guard—never a good thing. But half a job done was better than nothing, and anyhow, there was no other choice.

Though he'd done his fair share of hits in the past, he wasn't a professional. It was something he aspired to, but he hadn't made the move yet. There was a lot of money to be had in that vocation, but he was still practicing for that big day. He vowed to invest in a good silencer. It would come in handy right now.

He heard another footstep and peered around the back of the chair again. She was still not in sight. Probably putting her keys away or taking her shoes off or some such thing.

Then he saw a pair of eyes on the far wall of the foyer. They grew wide and he heard a gasp.

She had seen him in a mirror on the entryway wall. He cursed his stupidity as he sprang to his feet. He raised the revolver and aimed, his finger tightening on the trigger.

Too late. She had scurried up the hallway toward the kitchen. Fortunately, she never tried to run back outside. That was a good thing, and should work in his favor.

He knew the layout of the house. He'd arrived early, let himself in the back door, and spent a few minutes becoming familiar with the main floor of the dwelling. The hallway led into the kitchen and she was probably going for the back door. But he knew he could also circle into the kitchen from the living room, and that's where he headed.

He needed to get to her before she reached the back door or he would fail completely. That would be a first for him, and his employer would be none too pleased.

He couldn't let that happen, no matter what.

He leaped across the living room and into the kitchen. He raised the gun. She wasn't there and he frowned.

She must still be in the hallway. She hadn't gone upstairs or he would've known.

He eased across the room, both hands on his weapon, his eye sighting down the barrel, ready to finish the job that had started so poorly.

She wasn't in the hallway. Had she turned around and circled back? He spun, ready to fire, and moved to the living room door. She wasn't there.

He went back to the kitchen, stood still, and dropped his gun hand to his side. Listening. Listening for any telltale sound. All he heard was his own breathing and the beating of his heart.

He'd never been outsmarted before and wasn't about to let this one be the first to get the better of him. Especially not a woman. How humiliating.

Raising the weapon again, he tiptoed silently down the hallway, into the living room, then back to the kitchen.

That's when he saw the doorway, just inside the kitchen, near the entrance to the hall. It likely led to the basement. He crouched down. A small amount of light seeped out from underneath.

He sprang across the room and whipped the door open. The basement light was on.

He had guessed correctly. He heard a rustling, scrambling sound. She was down there somewhere. He hoped she wasn't armed. He would need to be careful.

He took the first step and crouched. He couldn't see her but his ears told him she was definitely down there somewhere. He took another step, then another, stopping briefly each time, his revolver ready to bring her down at a split second's notice. All he would need was one shot—he was that good.

He leaped down the last two steps and crouched on the concrete floor. Nothing. He swung around, the weapon and his body moving as one entity. One deadly killing machine.

Where was she? He frowned.

Across the room. Just behind a large treadmill. A door. It was closed, and he sprang toward it, hitting it fully with his shoulder. The door held. He tried again, and it crashed open, the frame shattered. The door bounced off the inner wall and sprang back. He stopped it with his hand and stepped inside, the revolver ready.

He had her now. There was no doubt.

His finger tightened on the trigger as he spun the weapon around the room. He stopped and pulled the trigger.

Once.

Twice.

Three times.

He cursed as the feet he had seen disappearing out the window were now out of sight.

He dashed forward and stepped onto the wooden box she'd used to reach the opening. He hefted himself up and pulled his torso outside, and there she was, to his left, racing across the back lawn. He would never be able to get to her now.

He had failed.

CHAPTER 17

Tuesday, 4:05 p.m.

IT TOOK LESS THAN five minutes for first responders to appear on the scene and secure the building after Annie called 9-1-1 from the house next door, where her best friend Chrissy lived. Officers searched the Lincoln house thoroughly before they declared it clear. The would-be murderer had fled.

Jake had returned home while the search was underway, and Hank arrived shortly thereafter.

Annie looked at her husband, sitting on the edge of the couch, his face still showing the horror he felt at the sudden discovery of his home surrounded by cops.

"I had no idea what was going on," he said. "Naturally, I feared the worst." He turned to Hank, standing in the doorway. "I went to fill up with gas, and when I got back ..."

"I think you should get a better lock for the back door, Jake," Hank said. "It looks like the guy was a pro."

Annie tried to control her trembling body. When she had first seen the killer in the mirror, she'd reacted almost without thought. Her first instinct was to get out of the house. As she dashed down the hallway, she saw him standing, a gun in his hand, and knew he meant business. She didn't have time to be afraid, but now, thinking back on her close call, she was terrified, and she still shivered all over.

"What confuses me the most is why," she said. "Is this related to the Shaft case, or something else?"

"What concerns me more is, the guy might be back," Jake said.

"We have to stop him before he does." Hank sat on the couch and looked at Annie. "Did you see his face?"

"Just briefly."

"Do you think you could recognize him again?"

Annie shook her head. "I don't think so. All I know is, it was a man, and he wore dark clothes."

"Hair color?"

"Not sure. I think he wore a cap. He wasn't especially big or small. That's about all I can tell you. I wanted to get out of there as fast as possible."

An investigator appeared in the doorway. "No unknown prints on the back door or the basement door, Hank. In fact, we checked the whole main floor, and nothing."

Hank bobbed his head up and down. "I expected as much. This guy might be a pro. He likely wore gloves."

"Do you think it might be Norton?" Jake asked.

Hank pursed his lips and looked at the ceiling a moment. "Perhaps. But for what reason?"

"Maybe he thinks Annie knows something?"

Hank looked at Annie. "Do you?"

Annie shrugged. "Not that I can think of." She paused. "I

think he might have been after both of us, and thought Jake would be here as well."

"If it was Norton, how would he know we were looking into the case?" Jake asked.

"Lisa Krunk," Hank said.

Jake looked confused. "Lisa Krunk?"

"From the interview she did with Maria Shaft. They've been running teasers all day. The complete story is scheduled for six, and your names were mentioned."

Annie's brow wrinkled in disgust. "That woman is always sticking her beak in where she's not wanted."

Hank nodded. "And a murder always catches everyone's attention." He looked at Annie. "Lisa might be a royal pain, but she's only doing her job as a reporter."

"So the whole city knows about this case now," Jake said.

"Afraid so," Hank said. "And if it was Norton, we have no way to connect the dots. Annie said he fired two, maybe three shots through the window, but no bullets were recovered. Assuming they didn't hit anything, they're probably halfway across the city. So with no bullets and no fingerprints, and since Annie didn't see his face ..." He shrugged. "We don't have much."

Annie glanced over as she heard footsteps on the stairs. In a moment, Matty poked his head into the living room. "Can I come out of my room now?"

Annie looked at Jake, then back at Matty. "Yes, but stay in the house."

Matty leaped onto the couch between Hank and Jake. "What's going on here, anyway?"

Everyone sat back and looked at Matty, unsure how to answer. Finally, Jake said, "Someone was in the house while we were away, but he's gone now, and everything's okay."

"How did he get in?" Matty asked.

"The back door."

Matty's face brightened. "Did you check for fingerprints?"

Hank grinned. "We checked. No prints."

Matty frowned. "What about the neighbors? Maybe somebody saw him."

"You might be right. We have officers checking up and down the street." Hank paused and looked intently at Matty. "Do you have any more ideas?"

"Not right now."

Hank looked at Annie. "I'll make sure officers watch the house at all times until we catch him."

"I hope it won't be long," Annie said.

"I suppose you have no new leads on the Shaft case?" Jake asked.

"Not yet. We're still hoping to find Norton's car. It has to be somewhere."

Annie turned to Hank. "It skipped my mind with all this going on and I forgot to mention it. We went to see Tammy Norton. It turns out she and her husband don't get along as well as she let on. We finally got her to admit ..." She paused and glanced at Matty. "Her husband ... doesn't treat her too well."

"Are you saying what I think you're saying?"

Annie nodded. "We saw some ... evidence on her face, and she admitted it."

Matty slid off the couch and wandered toward the kitchen. Annie watched him leave, and then leaned toward Hank and whispered. "She had a black eye and a bruise on her chin."

Hank sat back and crossed his arms, the fingers of one hand tickling his chin. "So, he's violent."

"At least, toward her," Jake said. "But she still covers up for him."

Hank looked at the floor, shaking his head slowly. "This case is getting more confusing all the time. I'm trying to piece everything together into some plausible scenario, but nothing fits. And I can't find anything that even remotely looks like a motive."

"What about that nine-ball tournament that shows Shaft and Norton had a relationship?" Annie asked. "Anything on that yet?"

"I have plans to go to the pub where the tournament was held. Talk to the organizer and any other people either one of them might've come into contact with."

"That should keep you busy for a while," Jake said.

Hank shrugged and stood. "I'm a detective and that's what detectives do. I have to take the boring jobs along with the rest." He grinned. "Besides, I have King to help me." He paused. "I haven't heard back from him yet, so I assume he doesn't have any earth-shattering news, but as soon as he returns, I'll set him to work again."

"And I plan on going over everything we know," Annie said as she stood and followed Hank to the door. "Maybe I'll come up with a new approach."

She had no idea what that approach would be, but there had to be an answer somewhere.

CHAPTER 18

Tuesday, 5:59 p.m.

JAKE SWITCHED on the television and stretched out on the couch, his back against the armrest. The story by Lisa Krunk was scheduled for 6:00, and though he was disgusted at the way she sensationalized every news report, it pertained to the case they were working on and he didn't want to miss it.

Matty lay on the floor, a cushion under his head. He laid his comic book aside and watched the final commercial before the evening news began.

Annie came into the room and sat in her armchair, placing a cup of coffee on the stand beside the chair. She leaned forward slightly, her hands in her lap, and looked at the TV, waiting for the broadcast to begin.

The Channel 7 Action News logo flashed, teasers ran, and music played as the anchor shuffled his papers, the camera zoomed in, and the newscast began.

"Our top story: The senseless murder of a Richmond Hill man yesterday has struck fear into citizens of this city. With the story, here's Lisa Krunk."

The scene showed a gurney, covered with a white sheet, being wheeled from an alleyway toward a waiting ambulance. Yellow tape could be seen in the foreground, flapping gently in the evening breeze.

The camera panned, showing a car parked awkwardly in the middle of the street, its door wide open, detectives and officers milling about everywhere, the entire area cordoned off. Lisa began her voiceover as the camera continued to display the crime scene.

"This city was shocked to hear of a murder late yesterday evening. Thirty-five-year-old Werner Shaft was gunned down, receiving several shots before finally succumbing to his wounds. The unknown assailant fled the scene, leaving police baffled by the killing. There didn't appear to be any witnesses to this tragedy."

Lisa's face appeared on television screens throughout the city, standing at the same scene, the area now cleared as if nothing had happened the day before. She continued.

"Today, everything's back to normal at the place where this grisly crime took place, but the owners of these establishments are on their guard. Police declined to comment earlier, but I have been told that, as of today, they have evidence pointing directly to one suspect."

A picture of a man appeared on the screen. Jake recognized the face from the photo in the police reports as Lisa continued.

"Thirty-three-year-old Michael Norton is wanted for the murder of Shaft. Norton is an ex-convict, sentenced several years ago for burglary, and subsequently spent time in federal custody."

The TV showed Lisa knocking on the door of the Norton house. The door opened a crack and then closed abruptly. Lisa turned around, the camera zoomed in on her, and she shrugged.

"The Norton family refused to comment, but sources state the family claims no knowledge of the whereabouts of this dangerous man. The refusal of Norton's wife to talk to me leads me to believe she's covering for her husband, and though there's no evidence against her, police are looking at Tammy Norton closely. She's certainly a person of interest in this case.

"Sources state it's only a matter of time before this dangerous man is apprehended, and he's believed to be nearby, possibly still in the immediate area.

"A search of the Norton residence this morning resulted in no further information on the fugitive's location, and his wife declined to state whether or not she knew of his plans and where he might be hiding."

Jake dropped his feet off the couch, sat forward, and pointed to the television. "She's making this stuff up," he said. "How can she draw a conclusion like that because Tammy Norton doesn't want to comment?"

"She's just being Lisa," Annie said.

"Sounds more like slander to me."

The television screen flickered and the scene moved to the inside of a house. Jake recognized Maria Shaft, sitting in a chair, the camera trained on her worried face. The view pulled back, revealing a man standing at her side. It was Rocky Shaft, his thick brows in a tight line.

Lisa continued.

"I spoke earlier with the wife of the victim, Maria Shaft, and the victim's brother, Rocky. Rocky had this to say:"

"We want that killer caught. If I get ahold of you, I'll break your worthless neck."

"Maria, what can you tell me about the relationship between your husband and the suspect, Michael Norton?"

"There's no relationship and there hasn't been for years. My husband was a good man and he didn't deserve this."

The scene changed to a shot of Lisa, standing in front of the police station, a smug look on her face as she spoke.

"My sources inside this building inform me Mrs. Shaft's statement is not true; there is in fact a relationship between the victim and Michael Norton, going back several years. The victim was Norton's accomplice in the burglary case, and both men spent some time in prison."

Jake tried to remain patient when a photo of him and Annie came on the screen and Lisa continued.

"Sources also confirm Lincoln Investigations, whom you will all recognize as being involved in several high-profile cases lately, have now turned their attention to this baffling mystery.

"Viewers will remember, the Lincolns, along with this reporter, were instrumental in bringing a killer to justice in recent history, and I'm willing to aid the police with my expertise in investigative journalism once again."

Annie almost choked on her coffee. "She's mighty high on herself."

Jake laughed. "She's a narcissist with an ego that just won't quit."

A photo of Norton came on the screen. It was his mug shot, taken several years ago when he was first arrested.

Lisa said:

"If you have seen this man, or have any knowledge as to his whereabouts, I urge you to contact the police immediately.

"I will be following this story closely, and will bring you breaking news as it happens.

"For Channel 7 Action News, I'm Lisa Krunk."

Jake switched off the television, leaned back, and said, "There wasn't much new there. Mostly Lisa blowing her own horn, but Rocky Shaft was pretty angry."

"We'd better find Norton before he does. Rocky

threatened to kill Norton, and I wouldn't be surprised if he tried."

Jake looked at Annie. "I wonder why she always mentions our names."

"So she can claim credit. Whether it's us or the police, she has a need to feel involved," Annie said. She sat back, took the last sip of her coffee, and set the cup on the stand. "I think she believes her own exaggerations."

"She doesn't seem like a nice woman," Matty said as he stood and wandered away.

Annie laughed. "From the mouth of babes."

"Even Matty can see right through her," Jake said. "But forget about her. We need to concentrate on finding Michael Norton."

"Let me sleep on it," Annie said. "I'll come up with something tomorrow."

Jake was pretty sure she would.

CHAPTER 19

Tuesday, 6:13 p.m.

HANK LOOKED UP AS Detective King approached his desk and flopped into a chair. The cop looked worn out, grumpy, and in need of a change of clothes—nothing unusual there.

"No luck today, Hank," King said. He yawned and leaned back, dropping one foot on the edge of Hank's desk. "Nobody has seen or heard from Norton in a while."

Hank set his pen down and sat back. He had hoped to hear some good news, anything they could run with, but in reality, he wasn't surprised. Norton was lying low, not dumb enough to hide out anyplace conspicuous.

At least he'd gotten away from King for most of the day. That was always good.

"Did you hit them all?" Hank asked, knowing what the answer would be.

"Every one. Some I had to track down at work, but I got to them all."

"Then you might as well go home for the night," Hank said, waving his hand. "I'm about done here myself, and then I'll be heading out."

King dropped his foot and leaned forward, poised to leave. "What's up for tomorrow?"

"If nothing else comes up we'll hit Smokie's Bar," Hank said. He told King about the tournament Shaft and Norton had been involved in. "We'll talk to the owner and see what he can tell us."

"Sounds like a lot of fun," King said dryly as he stood and headed away. "See you tomorrow, Hank."

Hank leaned over his desk again. He wanted to get the reports out of the way to clear the day tomorrow. He looked up again. King was on his way back.

"Diego wants to see us a minute."

Hank looked across the precinct floor. Diego stood in the doorway of his office looking their way. Hank tossed his pen down and pushed his chair back. He followed King into Diego's office.

The captain sat at his desk and motioned toward a chair. "Sit down."

Hank took the only free chair and stretched out. King stood by the end of Diego's desk, his arms crossed, a bored look on his face.

"Fill me in, guys," Diego said, looking back and forth between the detectives.

"Not much to tell, Captain," Hank began. "I'm still

hoping to find some sign of Norton, or his car at least, but he's burrowed himself deep."

Diego nodded and looked at King. "Nothing from me," King said, shrugging a shoulder. "Been out all day talking to anyone he knows. Came up empty."

The captain sat back. "So what you guys are telling me is you're at a dead end?"

Hank nodded. "Not quite. We have a couple more leads to follow up on."

"What about the guy who invaded the Lincoln house? Anything on him?" Diego asked.

"Nothing. But he seems like a pro. I have officers watching the house round the clock, so if he returns we'll nab him."

"What about you, King?" Diego asked with a deep frown. "Don't you have any CIs who might know of a hitman in the neighborhood?"

"I'll check in with them tomorrow," King said. "But most of my CIs aren't in the murder business. Mostly drugs and petty crime."

Diego sat back and combed at his bristling mustache with two fingers. "That's not the only reason I wanted to see you guys. I want to know what you think of Lisa Krunk's story." He motioned toward a small television, now turned off, sitting on a shelf along one wall. "Did either of you catch it? Lisa made a few pointed accusations. Any truth to them?"

"I caught the teasers earlier in the day," Hank said. "Rocky Shaft is pretty angry. Can't say I blame him. He's got to be under a lot of stress right now. Other than that, I didn't hear anything that excited me."

"Lisa is claiming Tammy Norton is harboring her husband, covering up for him," Diego said.

Hank sighed. "That's just Lisa. I can't find any evidence of that. Mrs. Norton wants her husband found. Says he's innocent, and the only way to prove it is to find him."

King snickered. "Of course he's innocent. They always are."

Captain Diego ignored King's comment and kept his eyes on Hank. "What about Maria Shaft's claim there was no relationship between her husband and Michael Norton?"

Hank laughed. "It's not quite the way Lisa made it sound, Captain. She left out some important information. A little clever editing on her part. I don't have much faith in Lisa's broadcasts no matter how convincing they sound."

Diego stared thoughtfully at Hank a moment before clearing his throat. "I want you to tell the Lincolns to back out of this one. They might be private detectives, but they're citizens, and there's already been an attempt on Annie's life. I don't need any more bodies."

"That sounds like a good idea, Captain," King said.

Hank frowned at King and then leaned forward. "They aren't going to want to do that, Captain. When their lives are threatened, they get more determined."

Diego removed his cap and brushed back his hair with one hand. His eyes narrowed and the muscles of his jowls worked. Finally, he dropped his cap back on, adjusted it in place, and spoke. "I realize you don't have the time to keep an eye on them, but make sure they stay out of the way. I've given them a lot of leeway in the past, and I'll admit, they've been helpful at times, but …"

"And they've been helpful this time too, Captain. Annie's the one who got Tammy Norton to admit her husband beats her up. I didn't see any evidence of that." Hank paused and took a deep breath, letting it out slowly. "I'll keep an eye on them, but I don't think we can tell them what they can and cannot do. As long as they stay within the law."

"Fair enough," Diego said. "But make sure they don't keep any evidence from you."

"They never do, Captain. They've always been forthcoming. I think their history shows that." He paused. "Why would they keep anything back? They not only want to see justice done, but they have clients to take care of. It's their job."

"I realize I can't keep them out of this entirely, but tell them to be careful. We already suspect Norton killed at least one person, and we know he beats his wife. If he's the one who made the attempt on Annie, either himself, or with a pro, then he needs to be stopped ASAP. He's proven himself to be a violent person."

"We'll get him," Hank said.

Diego dropped his elbows on the armrests and steepled his fingers under his chin. He didn't share his thoughts, but rather dismissed the detectives with a wave. "Go home now, guys. You can get back at it in the morning."

Hank stood. "I'll finish the reports then I'll be out of here." He turned to go. "Goodnight, Captain."

Diego waved again, his eyes buried in a file folder. "Good night."

King followed Hank from the office, crossed the quiet room, and went out the front door.

Hank returned to his desk and sat, pulling a file toward him. He looked at his watch. This was going to be an early night for a change. He would have time to drop by and see Amelia before going home, and he hoped to get an early start the next morning.

CHAPTER 20

DAY 3 - Wednesday, 8:35 a.m.

JAKE HUSTLED MATTY and Kyle out the front door of the house and into the Firebird. He glanced toward the patrol car parked at the curb. The same two cops had been there most of the night, keeping a close eye on the house.

One of the officers called Jake's phone from time to time, keeping in touch, reassuring them, and checking to see if everything was all right inside the house.

Jake started the vehicle and pulled from the driveway, stopping beside the cruiser. He rolled down his window. "You guys okay?"

The cop in the driver seat nodded. "All quiet last night. Everything all right in the house?"

Jake nodded, and the other cop looked over and stifled a yawn.

"Annie's making you guys a cup of coffee. She'll be out in a minute."

"Sounds good," the driver said, looking at his watch. "We still have a couple hours to go before some fresh guys get here."

Jake waved a hand and pulled away. He appreciated the watch put on the house, but didn't expect the would-be killer to return. Nonetheless, they had been threatened, and the safety of his family was his top priority.

North Richmond Public School was only two blocks from the house and Matty usually walked to school with Kyle, his best friend who lived next door to the Lincolns, but today Jake wasn't taking any chances.

He drove to the school, pulled in front, and escorted the boys to the door of the building. He waited until they were inside before returning to the car.

He opened the vehicle door and glanced around. It was a warm day, too warm for anything other than a t-shirt, and certainly too warm to be wearing a ski mask. And the man now approaching him from the rear of the car not only wore a ski mask, but the upraised pistol in his hand showed he meant business.

Jake dropped to the ground as the weapon spat lead. The bullet zipped over his head and through the open window of the car.

The second shot followed immediately, but by then, Jake had rolled to the side. He stumbled to the front of his vehicle on all fours. He heard footsteps, following, relentless. He dove to the opposite side of the car and looked around for some means of protection.

The vehicle wouldn't cover him for long. The assassin only needed one clear shot and it would be all over.

His first instinct was to run directly away from the car, toward the school, but his second instinct took over. There were kids that way. A lot of kids, and a stray shot could hit any one of them.

He took a chance and poked his head up. The gunman was at the front of the vehicle. One more step and Jake would be in the open, totally vulnerable.

He dove to the back of the vehicle as the shooter approached the side, the deadly weapon ready to fire at a split second's notice.

Jake sprang to his feet and raced across the street, running at an angle, praying the assassin wasn't adept enough to hit a moving target.

A bullet whined past his head and he ducked, hit the ground, and rolled behind a tree at the edge of the sidewalk. He was safe for a couple of seconds, but a quick glance around the tree trunk showed his assailant still approaching.

He turned and sprinted down the sidewalk, but in a moment the shooter was directly behind him. Another bullet whistled past, dangerously close. He was fully exposed, and now the gunman was running after him—that would throw off his aim, but how long would it be until a bullet found its mark?

People were on the sidewalk ahead of him as well as across the street. Many ducked out of sight when they heard the shots, most still in danger from a stray bullet.

He dipped to the left and ran toward the side of a house. That would be safer for him and everyone around, and he hoped there was no one behind the dwelling.

Keeping low, he reached the side of the house and glanced over his shoulder. His pursuer was still coming, never giving up, determined and deadly.

He dashed to the rear of the house and looked around for a weapon, but with only seconds to spare, there was no time to waste.

Should he circle the house? The killer might have the same idea and could turn back and cut him off. He made a quick decision and ran to the rear of the property. He hopped a small fence dividing it from the neighbor behind, racing along the side of the house toward the next street over.

Another shot exploded, this time flattening itself against the brick wall of the house, inches from his head.

This man was persistent and seemed to be determined.

Jake finally reached the street and he crossed over, ducked behind a tree, and glanced back. The shooter pursued.

An idea struck him. Carver Street, where their house was, was one block over, on the next street parallel to where he was. He whipped out his cell phone, found the last inbound caller, and hit redial.

"Everything okay?" the officer asked.

"It's Jake. I'm half a block away on foot and I'm being pursued by a gunman." He took another glance and crossed the front yard of the house, heading toward Carver.

"I'll be coming from beside the house to your left about three doors up," Jake spoke quickly into the phone. "And he's behind me."

"We're on it." Jake heard the car door open. The officers would be prepared.

He glanced back as he hopped the hedge between the two dwellings. The hitman was close. He had lost some ground as he made the call. The gunman stopped and leveled his weapon.

Jake ducked as the assailant fired, and the bullet missed its target.

He jumped to his feet, crossed the backyard at an angle, and ran up the side of the house. Carver Street was directly ahead. Just a few more seconds.

He hit the sidewalk, running fast, and crossed the street. A sideways glance showed the gunman but a moment behind.

Down the street, he saw the police cruiser parked in front of his house. The officers were out of the vehicle, heading toward him a step at a time, their guns drawn and ready. They'd seen him.

He ducked behind a tree and spun back around. The hitman had reached the sidewalk across the street, stopped, and then stepped into the street, sighting down the barrel of his weapon, directly at the tree where Jake waited.

He glanced to his left. The officers were fifty feet away, still approaching.

Forty feet.

Thirty feet.

The killer spun his head to the left and stopped short in the middle of the street.

"Put your weapon down," an officer yelled. "Now."

The gunman whirled to face the cops, crouched, and fired a shot. It missed, and the officer fired back, the bullet whining through the spot the shooter had occupied a split second before. The hitman leaped aside, sprang to his feet, and ran for cover, back the way he came.

Jake watched the officers pursue the maniac until they were out of sight.

Several minutes later, they returned empty handed.

The cops had called for backup. The surrounding streets would be thoroughly searched, but the would-be killer was undoubtedly long gone.

CHAPTER 21

Wednesday, 9:18 a.m.

ANNIE HAD HEARD gunfire coming from the street, and when she looked out the front window, she saw Jake standing on the sidewalk, the pair of officers dashing across the lawn of the neighbor's house. She was relieved to see Jake was unharmed, but his vehicle was nowhere in sight.

A few minutes later, Jake came in and explained what had happened. "Matty and Kyle are okay," he said. "They were safely inside the school before any of this started."

She heard the whine of sirens in the distance. More than one vehicle was approaching the neighborhood, and officers would immediately set up roadblocks and scour the area.

Annie was concerned at the brazen persistence of the gunman. He'd obviously done some research and known Jake would be dropping Matty at school. Or perhaps he'd assumed as much and had alternate plans. Either way, she believed the assassin would make another attempt. It was obvious he was after both of them.

Jake appeared to be unfazed by the alarming incident, but she knew he was concerned and wouldn't take this standing still. And neither would she.

"If you drive me to pick up my car," Jake said, "I'll run down to RHPD. I should fill out a report."

While Annie went to get her handbag and keys, Jake gave Hank a call to fill him in. When Annie joined Jake, he told her the detective was shocked and deeply concerned for their safety. Hank was doing an interview at the moment, but would soon be on his way back to the precinct and would meet them there.

They locked up the house, got into Annie's car, and headed out.

Officers already swarmed the neighborhood, cruisers and cops everywhere, stopping cars and canvassing houses in the area. An officer waved Annie down, and after a cursory glance through the window, they motioned her through.

Jake's vehicle was still where he'd left it. Someone had closed the driver-side door, and though it was the least of his worries, he was relieved to see it hadn't sustained any damage.

He drove it home, Annie following in her Escort. He left it in the driveway, got back into Annie's car, and turned to face her as she pulled out of the driveway.

"I think we should get you a vest," he said. "This guy's determined."

Annie glanced over at her husband. It would be a good idea if both of them wore bulletproof vests for now. Jake had one at home that had saved his life in an earlier case, and she would ask Hank if they had one small enough to fit her.

She turned her eyes back on the road. "I'll wear one if you wear yours," she said.

Jake agreed. "It's a deal. We'll talk to Hank."

In a few minutes, Annie pulled into the precinct parking lot and eased into one of the guest spots. She stepped from the vehicle and looked around, half-expecting to see the gunman waiting. He wasn't, and she and Jake went into the precinct.

Captain Diego watched them come through the front doors and called them over. He stood in the doorway of his office, his usual pleasant face twisted into a frown of concern. He smiled grimly and greeted them with a nod.

"I spoke to Hank yesterday about you two," the captain said. He folded his arms and leaned against the door frame. "As if it's not bad enough that someone's out to get you, we don't know who, or why."

"We're going to find out who," Jake said. "And why."

"I'm concerned about your involvement in this case," Diego said.

Annie put a hand on one hip. "We're already involved whether we like it or not," she said. "It's become personal."

"And dangerous," Diego said, his frown deepening.

Annie looked at Jake then back at the captain. "We'll be careful. We appreciate your concern, Captain Diego." She paused. "I have a favor to ask."

Diego raised his brows.

"Can I borrow a bulletproof vest?"

Diego chuckled. "Of course." He held up a finger. "Remember, these vests aren't bulletproof, just bullet resistant. You can still sustain some damage if you get hit, especially at close range."

"I'm aware of that," Annie said. "Jake can attest to that firsthand."

The captain glanced toward the door and Annie followed his gaze. Hank and King had come in, and Diego called to Hank.

The detective nodded, beckoned toward them, and then went to his desk. Annie thanked Captain Diego and they approached Hank.

"It appears the captain wants us to back off," Jake said.

Hank set his briefcase beside his desk, sat down, and leaned back in his chair. "And you don't want to, I assume?"

"We can't," Annie said, sitting in the guest chair. She leaned forward. "If we back off, we become easier targets."

"I'd better fill out a statement," Jake said. "While I do, Hank, can you fit Annie with a vest?"

"Sure," Hank said, standing. He motioned toward Annie and she followed him across the room, through a door, and into the lower level of the building.

She heard some muffled shooting; someone was in the firing range close by.

Hank selected a vest and handed it to her. "This should fit you. Do you know how to put it on?"

"I do."

"I'm not surprised."

Annie had worn a thin cardigan over her t-shirt and she

removed it, fastened the bulky vest in place, and put the cardigan over top. It was a little uncomfortable and rather awkward at first, but she felt safer.

"Make sure Jake wears his," Hank said.

Jake had finished with his statement when they returned to Hank's desk. The detective read it over. "There's not much here," he said to Jake.

"There's not a lot to tell. He wore a ski mask, so I didn't see his face, and I was too busy running to see much more."

Hank dropped the paper on his desk and sat back. "King and I came from Smokie's Bar. The owner attested Shaft and Norton knew each other. They were frequent visitors to the bar and entered all the tournaments. He confirmed that, as far as he knew, neither of their wives ever came with them."

"That fits with what both women told us," Annie said.

Hank nodded. "I also got a list of everyone else in the tournament, so between King and me, we'll see what they know about the relationship between Shaft and Norton. Or more important, where Norton might be hiding out." He shrugged. "It's a long shot, but it's about all we have right now."

"I'd love to get ahold of this guy that's been shooting at us," Jake said. "I'm sure he knows a thing or two."

"There's no proof it's related to this case," Hank said.

Annie spoke. "It is."

Hank pointed a finger at Jake and frowned. "You guys be careful."

Jake chuckled. "Of course, Hank. Have you ever known us to be anything but careful?"

"You've taken a chance or two in the past."

"Calculated chances."

"Just be careful," Hank said.

Annie stood. "See you later, Hank. We'll let you know if anything happens."

Hank called to them as they turned and headed for the doors. "And wear your vests whenever you're out of the house."

CHAPTER 22

Wednesday, 10:55 a.m.

HANK TURNED AND glanced across the precinct when he heard his name called. It was King, a rare look on his face, something halfway between a grin and a smirk.

He spun his chair to face the approaching detective. "Looks like you won the lottery."

"Maybe I did," King said, leaning against the desk. "One of my CIs might know who the shooter is. Won't tell me over the phone. Says he'll never get paid that way."

"Does your source know where to find him?"

"He says no, but he has a name." King shrugged. "It's a start."

Hank eyed the crass detective. King had never taken to the mundane matters, not excelling at the finer details of police work, but when it came to fitting in on the streets and obtaining inside dirt on local criminal activity, he was unsurpassed.

"Gotta go, Hank. I'll be back before long," King said and strode away.

Hank turned back to his desk. He'd been putting together a few notes for a hurried press conference. The local and regional news outlets demanded something, and Diego always did his utmost to keep the public aware of anything affecting their daily lives.

He gathered up his notes and went to the doorway of Diego's office. "All set, Captain."

When Hank and Diego stepped from the precinct doors, people were already gathered in front of the podium at the bottom of the steps. There were fewer reporters than usual, as little notice had been given, but Lisa Krunk could be seen at the front of the small group, Don at her side, the camera on his shoulder.

They descended the steps and Hank moved to the podium, consulted his notes, and cleared his throat.

"Thank you for coming." His eyes roved over the gathering. "I'll make a brief statement and then take questions."

He glanced at his notes again before speaking. "As you know, Monday evening, a brutal murder took place in this city. The victim was thirty-five-year-old Werner Shaft, a resident of Richmond Hill." Hank held up a photo. "This man, Michael Norton, is a suspect in this case, and I urge you all to publish or broadcast this picture. We think he's still somewhere in the city, but so far, he's eluded our search."

Hank looked at Lisa and continued, "In regards to a recent broadcast, we have no information leading us to believe the suspect's wife has any knowledge of his whereabouts." He paused. He didn't have much else to say. "This case is ongoing and I'll keep you up to date on any further developments."

Hank looked at Diego, then back at the crowd. "I'll take your questions now," he said, pointing to an upraised hand.

"Detective, it's my understanding Lincoln Investigations is involved in this case and there was an attempt on Annie Lincoln's life yesterday. What can you tell us about that?"

Hank hadn't wanted to broach that subject. He hesitated and then said, "We have yet to ascertain whether or not it's related to the Shaft murder."

The reporter persisted. "Do you have a suspect in that attempt?"

"Not yet. It's a priority for us, and everything is being done to ensure their protection and the safety of the public."

Lisa raised a hand and spoke. "Detective Corning, I understand Jake Lincoln was the intended victim in another shooting attempt today. Do you believe it's the same perpetrator?"

Hank nodded. "We believe it is, and we expect to make an arrest shortly." He leaned in to the mike. "You'll be notified when we do. Please note, we have no reason to believe the general public is in any danger." He picked up his notes. "That's all for now."

He turned from the podium and ignored further questions. He and Diego climbed the stairs and returned to the precinct as reporters moved away.

Hank turned to Diego. "We didn't have much for them."

"We had to give them something. That'll keep them quiet for a while." Diego headed for his office. "Keep me up to date," he called over his shoulder.

Hank went back to his desk and dropped his notes into the wastebasket. He sat, pulled into his desk, and thumbed through the files pertaining to the case. He was frustrated, finding it hard to come up with an approach.

He was relieved from his thoughts when the front door opened and King strode in, a triumphant look on his face. Hank watched the detective approach his desk and sit in the guest chair. King sat back, folded his arms, and stretched out.

Hank looked at him. "Well, are you going to tell me?"

"Punky Brown," King said.

"Punky Brown? Never heard of him."

King shrugged. "That's the name I got. Somebody hired him to kill the Lincolns."

"Did your CI have any info on his whereabouts?"

King brushed back his greasy hair and sat forward. "Apparently, this Punky Brown character is not known to a lot of people. Word is, he's trying to make a name for himself as a first-class hitman."

Hank frowned. "And how does your CI know him?"

King cleared his throat. "He's kind of in the same business. Not a hitman per se, more of an enforcer than anything else." He paused. "As far as I know he's never killed anyone. I wouldn't shelter a killer."

"And so your CI is eager to give up his competition?"

King grinned. "Something like that."

"Any idea how to find this guy?" Hank asked.

"No idea, but somebody must know something. Apparently, Brown's not all as good as he claims to be. My CI says he's too stupid to ever amount to anything, and Brown is more of a wannabe than anything else. Takes foolish chances. Doesn't plan ahead. Things like that."

"That could make him even more dangerous," Hank said.

"Maybe. But it should also make him easier to find."

Hank spun his chair around and wheeled over to Callaway's desk.

"What can I do for you, Hank?"

"Can you find me anything on a guy named Punky Brown?"

Callaway tapped a few keys on his keyboard. He squinted at the monitor, tapped some more, and frowned. "Not finding anything, Hank."

"It's probably an assumed name," Hank said. "Thinks it makes him sound tough."

"There're lots of guys named Brown in the system," Callaway said, still peering at his monitor. "All across the country."

"Give me a printout on any within a fifty-mile radius," Hank said. "It's a long shot, but we'll look into every one."

"Will do. I'll bring it over when I'm done."

Hank spun back to his desk and looked at King. "Does your CI know what Brown looks like?"

King shook his head. "He has no idea. He's never met him."

"All right. Leave it with me," Hank said. He slipped a sheet of paper from a file folder and handed it to King.

"Here's a list of everyone in the nine-ball tournament. See if you can find anything out about Shaft or Norton."

King sighed and took the sheet. "This should be a real exciting job," he said as he stood and sauntered away.

Hank called Jake's cell number. He figured Jake and Annie at least deserved to know the name of the guy who had tried to kill them.

CHAPTER 23

Wednesday, 11:36 a.m.

JAKE HUNG UP THE phone, went into the office, and dropped into a chair. Annie turned away from the monitor and leaned back. She looked curiously at her husband.

"Punky Brown," Jake said.

"Who's Punky Brown?"

"The guy who's taking shots at us," Jake answered. "Hank called me. Brown is a two-bit punk who thinks he's a hitman. King got the name from one of his CIs."

"Did they catch him?"

"No. The problem is, they don't know who he is or what he looks like. All they have is a name."

Annie dropped her elbows on the desk and clasped her hands together under her chin. "It's a start."

"Can you find anything on him?" Jake asked.

"Don't hold your breath on that. If Hank has no info, I

doubt if I can." Annie's brow tightened. "The bigger question is, who hired him?"

Jake stood and paced the office. If Brown was getting the word out about his services, then somebody had to know. But they had no contacts in that world—at least, none who would talk to him.

He stopped pacing and spun to face Annie. "I know who might be able to help. Sammy Fisher."

Annie chuckled. "It's worth a shot."

"I'll go see if I can round him up right away. Want to come?"

Annie looked at her monitor, then at the file folders opened on the desk in front of her. "I think I'd do better to stay here and see what else I can come up with."

"Suit yourself," Jake said, looking at his watch. "I should be back in lots of time to pick up Matty and Kyle." He turned and left the office, then poked his head back in. "If you go out, don't forget to wear your vest."

Annie assured him she would and he hurried to the basement. He pulled his own vest from a shelf, blew off the dust, and examined it. The covering had a hole in one spot, the padding indented where it had stopped a bullet not so long ago. He had been wearing it at the time, and it was a close call. He had no aspirations of seeing another hole in the vest. At least, not while he was wearing it.

He put it on over his t-shirt, with a button-down shirt over top, and then grabbed his keys and headed out.

Another cruiser was parked in front, a different pair of cops inside. He waved at them as he pulled from the driveway and spun up the street, turning his thoughts to Sammy Fisher.

Sammy was an enigma. Homeless by choice, he'd helped the Lincolns a couple of times in the past. He always avoided Jake's questions as to why someone obviously intelligent and well educated would choose a life on the streets.

There was more to Sammy than met the eye. He seemed to have contacts everywhere—in every alleyway, and behind every dumpster in the city. Every cardboard box converted into a home sheltered someone Sammy called a friend.

Jake turned onto Front Street and pulled over to the side, twenty feet short of where the overpass crossed Richmond River. He got out of the car, stepped down into a small ditch, and faced an embankment descending fifty feet to the gentle river below.

He climbed down a few feet, dipped under the overpass, and grinned. It looked like Sammy still lived there. What Sammy called "his castle" was nothing more than a ten by ten excavation, tunneled into the embankment where the ground met the underside of the overpass, tucked back behind the concrete pillars.

A dirt-brown tarp camouflaged the doorway, sheltering it from the elements, and made the quarters invisible to all except those who knew it was there.

Jake pulled the tarp aside, peeked into the darkness, and chuckled.

The ground was covered with strips of wood, neatly laid side by side, making a solid floor. The back wall was shored up with wooden posts, covered with a piece of drywall. His bed consisted of a thick blanket and an old pillow. A couple of pots hung from the ceiling, and a small shelf unit contained the rest of Sammy's meager possessions.

But Sammy wasn't there.

Jake dropped the tarp back in place, climbed down the embankment, and sat on a flat rock by the edge of the river. Unless Sammy had changed his schedule, he should be back soon. In the past, Sammy had usually scrounged in the morning, come home for lunch, taken a nap, and then scouted around until evening.

He gazed into Richmond River as it rolled gently by, heading south to Lake Ontario. He was determined to find Punky Brown, not only for his own safety, but also for the sake of his family. The relentless killer was unpredictable and seemed desperate, and that made him dangerous.

"Detective Jake, what're you doing here?"

Jake glanced down the bank. A man in scruffy jeans, a baggy t-shirt, and a tattered baseball cap was heading his way. He held a well-used grocery bag in one hand and he waved with the other.

Jake stood and grinned. He took a step forward and held out his hand. "Sammy. Long time."

Sammy shook the offered hand and looked at Jake with clear blue eyes framed by a leathered face. The tip of his shaggy beard rubbed against his shirt as he spoke. "Good to see you again, Jake. What brings you to my humble abode?"

"I need your help again, Sammy."

"Anything for a friend," Sammy said as he kicked aside a soda can with a tattered running shoe and pointed toward the rock. "Have a chair."

Jake took a seat as Sammy dropped down on the grass and stretched his legs out, leaning back against his hands. "How's Detective Annie?"

"Annie's doing great. She mentions your name from time to time. Wondering how you're doing."

"I'm getting by." Sammy crossed his legs at the ankles and looked up at Jake. "What can I do for you?"

"I need to find a guy named Punky Brown. Apparently, he's a wannabe hitman, and he's been taking shots at Annie and me."

Sammy looked into the river and squinted. "I haven't heard the name before." He looked back at Jake. "What's he look like?"

"That's the problem. Nobody knows."

"Somebody knows," Sammy said.

"With your contacts and undying charm, I'm hoping you can find out something."

Sammy popped his cap off and brushed back his long, straggly hair with a hand. He put his cap back on. "I expect I can, Jake. Leave it with me and I'll talk to my street family."

Jake reached into his shirt pocket and pulled out a cell phone. "Here's a burner phone. Call me when you get anything."

Sammy took the phone and looked at it. "You're going to have to remind me again how to work these things. It's been awhile. The battery died a long time ago in the last one you gave me."

Jake gave Sammy some quick instructions on how to make a call. "My cell phone number is already in there," he said.

"The battery's good for a few days if you don't use it much."

"I don't have much use for one of these gadgets," Sammy said, dropping it into his shirt pocket. "I'll only be using it to call you, I expect."

"I hope to hear from you," Jake said as he stood. "I'd like to chat awhile, but I want to get back to Annie. Make sure she's okay."

"That's all right," Sammy said. "I don't have time to chat either. I have to find Punky Brown."

CHAPTER 24

Wednesday, 12:01 p.m.

ANNIE TOOK the last bite of her sandwich, put the plate in the sink, and started a pot of coffee. She put together a lunch for Jake and slid it into the fridge; he'd be hungry when he got back. She poured a cup of coffee, went into the office, and sat, staring blankly at her notes and sipping her drink. She didn't have a whole lot of ideas.

She was startled out of her thoughts when the phone on the desk rang. The caller ID was unknown and she picked it up. "Lincoln Investigations."

The caller hesitated. She heard light breathing, then, "This is Michael Norton."

Annie spun her chair around and looked at a piece of electrical equipment on a shelf behind her. The glowing red light assured her the call was being recorded. She turned back to the desk.

"This is Annie Lincoln." She fumbled for words, unsure what to say. "Where are you, Mr. Norton?"

Another hesitation. "I can't tell you that, but I ... I've been watching the news. They've got it all wrong. I'm not a murderer, Mrs. Lincoln."

"Then why don't you turn yourself in and clear your name?"

"Because I wouldn't last a day. I'd be killed like Werner Shaft was."

"Killed? By who?"

"I can't tell you that either. I can only tell you I'm innocent and I want you to prove it."

"If you're innocent, Mr. Norton, my husband and I will do whatever we can, but we have nothing to go on. I'll need your complete participation and you'll have to tell me everything."

There was a pause on the line, silence for so long Annie thought the caller had hung up.

"Are you still there?" she asked.

"I'm here." A deep breath and then, "I can tell you this. Werner Shaft, his brother Rocky, and I, were involved in a heist a few months ago. It was drug money. Rocky got wind of a big deal going down, so we teamed up and intercepted the money. We agreed to put it away for two years. Not touch it until everything blew over."

"So you think they found out who did it and they're after all three of you?" Annie asked.

"No. They had no idea who it was." Norton sighed. "But I believe Rocky got antsy for the money. He was impatient and was always after us to split it up. We refused. I believe he killed his brother and now he's after me. He's greedy that way. He wants it all for himself and he doesn't want to wait."

"But to kill his own brother?" Annie said.

"Worse things have taken place over money." He sighed again. "I wish I'd never gotten involved with those two. They were both bad news from the start. As you probably know, Werner and I did some time in prison together. It was through his carelessness we got caught, and I should've stayed as far away from both of them as I could."

"Mr. Norton, someone hired a hitman to kill my husband and me. Was it you?"

"Why would I do that? I want you to prove my innocence. I'm tired of running for my life. If it means going back to prison for the heist—fine, but I'm not going down for murder."

"And now you think Rocky Shaft is determined to kill you?"

"Probably. And now he's after you to keep you from finding out the truth."

"What about the evidence against you?" Annie asked.

"What evidence?"

"A shell casing with your prints on it."

Norton chuckled. "Planted. It wouldn't have been hard for Rocky to get ahold of that at one time or another. Probably took it right out of my gun. We hung around from time to time. Had a few beers together, things like that. He had a lot of opportunity."

"There was a witness that identified your car."

"Again, not so hard. My wife was babysitting that night

and I was at home. My car was parked in the driveway. He could easily have borrowed it without me knowing. Did the witness get the license plate number?"

"No, just the make and model."

"Then it could've been another car the same as mine. Possibly picked it up somewhere. Or borrowed it for the occasion from an unsuspecting person."

"Why didn't he kill you as well, or at least attempt to?" Annie asked.

"That wouldn't serve his purpose. He was using me as a patsy for Shaft's murder. Kill two birds with one stone, and then grab the money."

"What about your wife?" Annie asked.

"Tammy doesn't know anything about this at all."

"We talked to Tammy, Mr. Norton. She finally admitted you assaulted her on occasion."

Norton sighed. "We argued a lot and sometimes things got physical. I'll admit that, but there're a few marks on me as well."

"Why should I believe that?"

"You don't have to. It's unfortunate, yes, but it has nothing to do with any of this."

"Fair enough," Annie said. "But how am I going to prove your innocence?"

"By proving Rocky Shaft's guilt."

"Of course, but all the evidence is stacked against you. Nothing against him."

"There has to be something."

"Mr. Norton," Annie said, "at the beginning of our

conversation, you said you feared for your life. But if Rocky only wants to frame you for murder, why the fear?"

"Because, like you said, all the evidence is stacked against me. With me dead, and perhaps my body buried somewhere forever, the case will be closed, and my guilt will be proven as far as the police are concerned."

"So Rocky frames you, you disappear, and it's game over. Case closed."

"Exactly."

Annie had a lot to think about now. Assuming Michael Norton was being totally truthful with her, she needed to find some evidence against Rocky Shaft. That was like fighting an uphill battle, with everyone convinced Norton was the murderer.

"Leave it with me," she said. "I'll see what I can come up with."

"One favor, Mrs. Lincoln?"

"Yes?"

"Leave my wife out of this. I don't want her to be concerned for my safety."

"I'll see what I can do."

"I'll pay your fees once you clear me. Don't worry about that."

"We're already being paid by Maria Shaft to look into this."

"Yes, I know. I saw that on the news, but it's worth it to me if you clear my name."

"I'll do my best," Annie said.

Norton thanked her and hung up. She put the phone

down thoughtfully. This was an interesting development indeed.

She picked up the phone again and called Hank's cell.

"Detective Hank Corning."

"Hank, I got a phone call from Michael Norton. He claims he's innocent." She gave him a brief rundown on the conversation. "I recorded it and I'll get a copy to you immediately."

Hank whistled. "That could put a whole new light on things. Hold on to it and I'll pick it up as soon as I can."

"I'll make a copy right now and have it ready," Annie said.

CHAPTER 25

Wednesday, 12:49 p.m.

AS SOON AS JAKE arrived home, Annie stepped into the living room and called him into the office. He could tell something was up by the look on her face.

He followed her in, eased into the guest chair, and sat dumbfounded as she played back the phone call from Michael Norton.

"I've got a copy ready for Hank," she said. "We'll see what he makes of it."

Jake sat quietly a moment, trying to digest what he'd heard. "It all sounds logical," he said at last. "And if it's the whole truth, then Rocky Shaft has covered his tracks pretty well."

"I'm sure he slipped up somewhere. We have to find out where," Annie said thoughtfully, and then her face brightened. "How's Sammy?"

"He's good. He sends his greetings. He's still living in the same castle, and he says—" His voice trailed off, interrupted by the ringing of his cell phone. It was Sammy Fisher.

"I have some good news for you, Detective Jake."

Jake put the phone on speaker. "Already?"

Sammy chuckled. "I've been living out here a long time," he said. "I make it my business to get to know people, and I know how to ask subtle questions. I knew exactly who to turn to for answers this time."

"What did you find out?" Jake asked.

"You're right about Punky Brown being a two-bit hood. He's not shy about making it known he aspires to be a hitman. People I talked to said he just got out of prison, where he claimed to learn a thing or two. He's been putting the word out among the darker criminal elements—you want somebody done? Call Punky." Sammy laughed. "Sounds like a cheap business card."

Jake waited patiently until Sammy decided to get to the point.

"Folks tell me he hangs around a place called Smokie's Bar a lot?"

"Smokie's Bar?"

"You know the place?"

"Sure do," Jake said. "The victim and the suspect hung around there as well. That must be where the killer got in touch with him."

"I've been playing around with the phone," Sammy said. "I figured out how to take a picture."

"Tell me you got a shot of Brown."

"Yup. Sure did. And I figured out how to send it to you."

Jake heard breathing as Sammy paused, then said, "Tell me if you get it."

A moment later, Jake said, "Got it." He turned the phone so Annie could see the photo of a man, standing with a cue in one hand, watching someone take a shot at the pool table.

The photo was taken from several feet away, but Brown would be recognizable anywhere. His large nose and gaunt, sunken cheeks were most prominent, with his dark, ragged goatee a sharp contrast to his nearly bald head. He wore a faded denim jacket and dark pants.

Annie squinted at the phone. "It could be him. I didn't see him well enough to be sure."

"Thanks, Sammy," Jake said into the phone. "Great shot. I owe you one."

"You don't owe me. I'm glad to help. Just catch the guy who's been shooting at my friends and I'll be well paid."

"I'll let you know what happens, Sammy," Jake said. "We have to get together sometime soon. And Annie sends her greetings."

A chuckle came from the phone. "You know where I live."

Jake hung up and stood to his feet. "Brown might still be at Smokie's. I'll be back soon." In two long strides he was out of the room, heading for the front door before Annie could say a word.

In a moment he was back, a crooked grin on his face. "Do you know where Smokie's Bar is?"

Annie found the printout in her file and wrote down the address. "Be careful," she said, handing it to him. "Maybe you should call Hank."

"If I find the guy, I'll call him," Jake said as he charged from the room.

He raced from the house and jumped in the Firebird, and in a few minutes he pulled up half a block away from Smokie's Bar. He stepped out, walked up the sidewalk, and stopped in front of a windowless building. A rustic, wooden sign above sported the name of the establishment. A notice on the door promised half-price beer all morning.

Jake tugged open the large wooden door and stepped cautiously inside. The last thing he wanted was to be seen by Punky Brown, if the killer was still here.

He was greeted by a dimly lit, smoke-filled room. An endless bar ran along the near wall, a vast array of spirits displayed behind. Peanut shells and sawdust littered the floor. Most tables sat empty, some occupied with people in various stages of inebriation. Three or four patrons perched on barstools, hanging over their drinks. Smoke burned his eyes. Lively country music filled his ears.

At the far end of the large room, hanging lights lit up a handful of pool tables. Players leaned in, and well-aimed cues stroked the balls. They spun across the table, colliding with a click, click, some thudding into pockets.

Several bystanders sat bug-eyed, engrossed in the games, letting out occasional howls at a shot gone wrong, or a chorus of cheers when one went right.

Jake nodded at the bartender and eased closer to the pool tables. As far as he could tell, Brown was not there. No one paid him any attention as he moved a few steps closer and looked around.

Brown was gone.

He spun back and approached the bartender. "I'm looking for Punky Brown."

The proprietor wiped his hands on his off-white apron, squinted across the room, and shrugged. "He was here a minute ago. Guess he just left."

Jake looked around for the men's room, spied the sign at the far side, and strode across the room. He pushed the door open and stepped inside. No one was there.

He turned back and headed for the entrance, waving his thanks to the bartender as he strode by. He hurried out to the sidewalk and looked both ways. An old man hobbled up the street to his left, a couple of women to his right.

The sound of a motorcycle being kick-started caught his ears. He turned toward the sound and saw a familiar denim jacket, fifty feet away, past the old man.

It was him.

It was the guy who had tried to kill Annie and him, and he was getting away.

Jake's long legs sprang into action and he raced down the sidewalk as the bike eased forward. Five seconds later, his big hand had a fistful of denim, dragging the rider from the motorcycle. The bike went down and spun in front of an oncoming car. A horn blared and the vehicle swerved in time.

Jake dragged the man to his feet and whirled him around. His baseball cap soared away, revealing a bald head, a gaunt face, and cold green eyes, widening with recognition.

It was Punky Brown, and he was reaching under his jacket.

Jake grasped him by the wrist and yanked his arm back,

and a pistol clattered to the asphalt. Punky looked down at the weapon, then back up at Jake, his face contorted with anger. He struggled in vain to free himself from the viselike grip now holding both arms.

"Let me go," the killer demanded through gritted teeth, his eyes burning with hatred.

Jake spun Punky back around, twisted his arms behind his back, and held them solidly in place with one hand. With the other, he did a quick frisk, checking for more weapons.

"You're under arrest," Jake said, forcing him to the sidewalk, facedown. He held Punky solidly in place with a knee on his back, slipped out his cell phone, and called Hank's number.

"I have our wannabe hitman," Jake said when Hank answered. He gave the cop a quick briefing.

Hank was amazed and almost speechless. When he recovered, he said, "I can't come right now, but I'll contact dispatch and get the closest car there immediately. I'll see you at the precinct. Don't let him get away."

Jake grinned. "He's not going anywhere."

CHAPTER 26

Wednesday, 1:41 p.m.

HANK SLID HIS chair back and watched as Punky Brown was led into the precinct. The would-be killer had a sullen, defiant look on his face. His chin jutted out, his eyes darting furiously about the room as if looking for an escape route.

Hank stood and intercepted the procession. "Take him to interview room one," he said to the officer holding Brown firmly by the arm. "I'll be right in."

Punky glared at him briefly, then looked away as the officer marched him toward the back of the precinct.

Hank turned and grinned at Jake, a couple of steps behind. "Nice job."

"It was him or us," Jake said. "I had no choice."

"Annie'll be pleased."

"I called her on the way over. She's happy she doesn't have to wear the vest anymore. Frankly, I am too." He slugged himself in the chest. "Can't wait to get this thing off."

Hank chuckled. "Let's see what I can get from this guy," he said and turned to Detective King, who had wandered over. "Does he look familiar to you?"

King shook his head. "Never seen him before."

Hank led the way across the floor and down a hallway at the back of the large room. He pushed open a door and turned to Jake. "You can watch from here."

Jake went inside and King followed Hank into an adjacent room. The walls were bare, painted an off-white. A camera hung in one corner, pointed toward the center of the room. It would record everything said and done.

To their left, the upper half of the wall consisted of a large two-way mirror. Jake would be watching with interest from the other side.

Punky Brown sat on a bench on the far side of a metal table, facing the mirror, his hands cuffed to a ring embedded in the tabletop. He glanced up briefly as the detectives entered, his surly expression unchanged.

King stood at the end of the table, spread his legs, and crossed his arms. Hank pulled back one of the chairs on the near side, dropped a file folder on the table, and sat down. He stared at the suspect. Punky stared back, his chin in the air.

Hank opened the folder, leafed through it casually, and then looked back up. "What's your name?"

No answer.

"According to your driver's license, your real name is Francis Spankly." Hank grinned up at King. "Not the kind of name you would expect from such a tough guy as this."

King leaned over the table and glared at Spankly. "The

thing is, he's not so tough without a gun in his hand." The cop straightened up and laughed. "Are you, Mr. Spankly?"

The suspect attempted to jump to his feet, the cuffs stopping him from getting more than halfway. He glared up at King, hatred in his eyes. The detective put both hands on the suspect's shoulders, forcing him back down. "Stay there, punk."

Hank leaned in. "Who hired you to kill the Lincolns?"

Spankly spoke for the first time. His squeaky high-pitched voice came out as a whine. "I don't know them."

"Annie Lincoln knows you," Hank said. "She can identify you as the man who entered her home, attempting to kill her."

Spankly looked around the room, avoiding eye contact. "It wasn't me. Probably somebody who looks like me."

King laughed. "Nobody looks like you, Spankly."

Hank knew lying to a suspect about evidence often got results, and he had no qualms about it in this case. "We have a slug from your pistol. As soon as ballistics compares it to your gun, we've got you."

"I lent my gun to somebody. Must've been him."

Hank glanced at the folder in front of him. "You fired on officers when you tried to kill Jake Lincoln. We have shell casings with your prints on them. That puts you at the scene."

Spankly glared at Hank a moment, his eyes narrowed, then he looked away and was silent.

Hank leaned back. "We all know it was you, Spankly. But here's the good thing. Maybe because you're so inept, or maybe from sheer luck, but as far as we know, you never killed anyone."

Spankly squeaked again, "That's right. I never killed nobody."

"Then all you have to do is tell us who hired you to kill the Lincolns."

The suspect stared silently toward the mirror as if seeing right through it, his face flushed with anger—or was it fear? Or both?

King leaned in again, grabbed Spankly by two hands full of denim, and pulled him from his seat. The cuffs reached their limit and clunked against the metal ring. King glared down into the cold green eyes from a distance of six inches. "You're going down for two counts of attempted murder if you don't talk to us." King let go and Spankly dropped back into his seat.

"You're not allowed to do that," Spankly said, a sullen look on his face.

King shrugged. "That's nothing. Wait until I get started."

Hank leaned forward and spoke gently. "I think it would be safer for you if you talk to us." He jerked a thumb toward King. "Detective King is kind of hard to control sometimes."

The door opened and an officer poked his head in, a sheet of paper in his hand. He gave it to Hank and went back out, closing the door behind him.

Hank studied the paper, smiled, and looked back at Spankly. "Says here you just got out of prison. Paroled for good behavior. That's hard to believe, but anything's possible." He laid the paper carefully on the table and leaned in. "Here's the thing, Spankly. I could put you away right now for parole violations. Consorting with known ex-cons. Carrying a concealed weapon. That would give you an automatic three more years."

"I say let's do it and be done with this guy," King said.

A hint of fear appeared in Spankly's eyes. The cuffs tinkled as he fidgeted with his hands.

"Last chance before I turn you over to King," Hank said. "Who hired you?"

"I don't know," Spankly said.

King leaned down again. "How can you not know?"

"I didn't see him."

Hank lifted a brow. "Then how did he hire you?"

"I got a phone call. Offered me five large to off the two of them."

"And how did you get paid?"

Spankly shrugged. "Didn't yet. After the job's done."

King laughed. "You're a real businessman, aren't you?"

"He said he knew me from prison. He dropped some names and it seemed like I could trust him." Spankly's head swung back and forth between Hank and King. "He said he would call me again when the job was done and arrange for payment."

"And you have no idea who it was?" King asked.

Spankly shook his head violently. "No idea."

"You'd better not be lying. If you are, we'll know, and you'll find out pretty quick we know." King leaned in close to reinforce the threat.

"I ain't lying," Spankly whined. "And I didn't kill nobody."

"You're sure it was a man?" Hank asked.

Spankly nodded vigorously.

"What was his voice like?"

"Normal voice, I guess."

"Like yours?" King asked, and then threw his head back and laughed.

Spankly said nothing, his eyes burning with renewed hatred.

Hank stood, opened the door, and stepped out into the hallway.

"Don't go anywhere," King said, laughing again, and followed Hank from the room.

Jake turned as Hank opened the adjoining room and stepped inside. The cop glanced through the glass. Spankly sat quietly, his head down, his hands clasped together.

"It's too bad we couldn't find out who hired him," Hank said. "But at least we know he's the one who tried to kill you. You two should be safe."

"Safe for now," Jake said. "But whoever hired him might find another way."

Hank nodded. "Unfortunately, you might be right."

CHAPTER 27

Wednesday, 3:27 p.m.

ALFIE OWENS ALWAYS protected his little sister—from other boys. But when no one else was around, Amber was the subject of as much torture and teasing as any eight-year-old could muster.

And like most boys he knew, he was quickly becoming an expert at making girls mad.

Amber, a year younger, was entrusted to his care each day as they walked home from school. This day was no different from any other.

Amber walked ahead, stepping carefully on each railway tie in perfect rhythm, one foot, and then the other, counting as she went.

One, two, three, four, five,
Once I caught a fish alive.
Six, seven, eight, nine, ten,
Then I let it go again.

Alfie stopped and crouched down. He had spied a small tree branch by the side of the tracks. He picked it up, grinned, and used it as a prod to hurry his sister along.

It didn't take her long to get tired of it. She spun on her heel, put her hands on her hips, and faced her bully brother. "Alfie Owens, if you don't stop that I'm going to tell Dad and he'll give you a good lickin'."

Alfie laughed. "I doubt that. We all know you get mad a lot about nothing. Who's gonna believe you?"

Amber moved closer, her eyes flaring, and grabbed for the branch. Alfie laughed, backed away, and stuck out his tongue. "Scaredy-cat."

She stopped and glared. "I'm not a-scared of you," she said.

"Maybe I'll tie you to the railroad tracks and let a train run over you," he said, with as mean a face as he could muster. "Then you'll be afraid."

Amber stuck her nose in the air. "Leave me alone." She spun around and marched away from her tormentor.

It wasn't in him to quit. In three quick steps he held Amber's long auburn ponytail in his fist. He tugged, not too hard, but none too gently.

She'd had enough for one day.

She reached up and freed her hair from his grasp with a tug and a toss of her head, and then spun around. She reached to push him away, but he stepped back. She stopped and crossed her arms as he taunted her. "Scaredy-cat. Scaredy-cat."

Amber's eyes flared and she stepped closer, but Alfie turned and loped ahead. She followed, angry now, not afraid of the bully.

A few steps in front of her, Alfie stopped short. The look on his face made her forget her anger as she followed his gaze toward the row of bushes along the side of the tracks.

Her mouth dropped open and her eyes widened. She brought her hands to her face, covered her eyes, and peeked carefully between her fingers at the startling sight in front of them.

Alfie moved in a step. The branch in his hand no longer served as a torture device, but was now being used to prod at the foot of the man who lay on the ground beside a bush.

Alfie crouched down and looked a little closer. He was pretty sure the man was dead. The only other person he'd seen dead before was his grandmother, and that was a long time ago. But his grandmother hadn't had flies buzzing around his head like this guy did.

And Grandmother hadn't had blood all over her like this guy did.

Alfie looked up at Amber. She stepped back, her face still turned toward the body, her eyes clamped shut, her arms wrapped around herself.

He stood and turned toward her. "It's a dead body," he said. "Amber, don't you wanna see the dead guy?"

Her eyes remained sealed and she shook her head vigorously.

"Scaredy-cat," he said.

She turned her back on him as he crouched and continued

his visual examination. The man's eyes were open, staring at the sky, but Alfie was pretty sure the guy couldn't see anything.

"I'm afraid," Amber said, her voice quivering. "We'd better tell a grown-up."

"Scaredy-cat," he said, continuing to eye the body curiously. "The guy's dead. He can't hurt nobody."

Amber walked away.

He crept up behind her and yelled, "Boo," and she jumped, spun toward him, and glared.

He leaned in and laughed. "Scaredy-cat."

Amber turned and walked away, her head high.

He sighed, stood, and followed her.

Amber stopped. "There's a house," she said, pointing. "Maybe there's somebody home."

They were less than twenty feet from an access lane running from the tracks, past a house, and to the street beyond.

She led the way, Alfie following, across the back lawn to the house. He stepped past her, climbed up on the back porch, and banged on the door.

An old woman finally answered, a curious frown on her face. She was at least as old as Alfie's mom and he figured she must be at least thirty-five. Maybe more.

Alfie looked her in the face, turned sideways, and pointed toward the tracks. "There's a dead guy back there. I ain't afraid but my sister is."

The woman frowned, looked at Alfie, and then looked at Amber, who was furiously nodding her head. "There really is," Amber said. "He lies a lot but he's telling the truth this time. I saw it too."

The woman looked back and forth between the two kids and then raised her eyes toward the back of the property. She turned, slipped on a pair of shoes, and stepped out onto the back porch. "Show me," she said, her tone revealing she wasn't certain whether or not to believe the far-fetched story.

Alfie marched off, leading the way. Amber stayed close at the woman's side as they followed him across the lawn and up the lane. He stopped and pointed.

The woman gasped, took a step back, seized Amber by the arm, and half-dragged her to the house.

Alfie took a last glance at the man on the ground and then turned and followed, swishing the stick through the air and wondering if all girls were scaredy-cats like these two.

CHAPTER 28

Wednesday, 3:54 p.m.

RHPD WAS NOTIFIED when the 9-1-1 call came in, and cruisers were dispatched immediately to secure the scene. Hank was informed, and by the time he and King pulled to the shoulder of the road behind a cruiser, its lights still flashing blue and red, the CSI van had already arrived.

The access lane leading to the tracks was taped off, and the main focus of attention seemed to be near a group of bushes, down the lane, along the side of the railroad tracks.

The coroner's van pulled in behind Hank's vehicle, and Nancy Pietek stepped from the passenger side. She joined the detectives. "Lovely afternoon, Hank, King," she said.

"Nice day to be alive," Hank answered.

King nodded, grunted, and said nothing.

The small group went up the lane, where investigators did what they do best. Trace evidence was being photographed, collected, and documented. Most of it would be meaningless, but the search for any elusive piece of telltale evidence would be thorough.

Hank approached Rod Jameson, lead CSI. "What do we have?" he asked, glancing at the body on the ground a few feet away.

Jameson consulted his clipboard. "A thirty-three-year-old male. Looks like he was shot in the chest. I'll defer that to Nancy. According to his driver's license, his name's Michael Norton."

Hank whistled. "Michael Norton?" He moved closer to the body and leaned over. There was no mistake; the pale white face was that of Michael Norton. The body lay flat on its back, facing upwards, the arms resting at each side. He looked like he might be sleeping, except his eyes were open, and he was very, very dead.

Nancy stepped over beside Hank and crouched down. She pulled aside the red plaid shirt, soaked with crimson, and made an examination of his chest wound.

"Gunshot wound to the heart," she said. "Small-caliber weapon." She pointed to the shirt. "Appears to be gunshot residue on the front of the shirt. As close as I can guess right now, he was shot from a distance of eighteen to twenty-four inches."

"Close up and personal," Hank said.

Nancy rolled the body slightly and examined the back. "Livor mortis shows he might've been killed here, or dropped here within a few minutes of death." She pointed to a light, purplish discoloration of the skin. "See how the blood has begun to settle. It starts to pool a few minutes after death and congeals after a few hours."

Jameson had come over, listening to Nancy's report. "It makes sense he was killed elsewhere, Hank," he said, pointing to the lane. "We found evidence the body was dragged from over there. And there are trace amounts of blood on the ground. That would indicate he was dead already."

"Or at least, mortally wounded," King added.

"I'd say he was already dead at the time the body was deposited here," Nancy said. "The shot would've killed him immediately."

King turned to Jameson. "Probably brought here in a vehicle. Any tire tracks?"

Jameson shrugged. "They're still looking closely at that, but the ground is hard. It's possible, but unlikely."

"Time of death?" Hank asked Nancy.

"Rigor mortis hasn't started to set in," Nancy replied. "I'd put the approximate time of death at two to three hours ago."

"So he was dumped here in broad daylight," King said.

Nancy nodded. "Almost certainly."

Hank crouched a little lower and rolled the body halfway over. "Looky here," he said. "He's carrying a weapon." He pulled a pair of surgical gloves from his pocket, worked them on, and then carefully removed a pistol from behind the back of the victim's belt. He held it up.

"A thirty-eight-caliber revolver," King said.

"Werner Shaft was killed by a thirty-eight," Hank said. He stood and turned to Jameson. "Better bag this."

The weapon was placed in an evidence bag, sealed, and labeled.

Hank crouched down again and patted the pockets of the victim's pants.

"We removed his wallet," Jameson said. "And we found a cell phone in his front pocket."

Hank stood. "Where's the phone?"

Jameson turned away and returned a moment later with an

evidence bag containing a cell phone. Hank removed it carefully. "It's not locked," he said. A moment later he looked up at King. "Last call was to Annie Lincoln. Twelve thirteen p.m." He dropped it back into the bag and handed it to Jameson. "Looks like he was killed not long after he made that call."

"So, if this guy killed Shaft," King said, "who killed him—and why?"

"Good question," Hank said and turned to Jameson. "Who found the body?"

"A couple of kids."

"Kids?"

Jameson pointed. "They're waiting in the house over there. They were walking the tracks on their way home from school, and there he was."

"Are their parents around?"

"The mother's on her way here from work. Father couldn't come."

Hank motioned to King. "We'd better go talk to them."

They walked to the house, where Hank tapped on the back door. He introduced himself and King when a woman answered. She led them into the kitchen and motioned toward a boy and a girl sitting at the kitchen table, hunched over steaming hot chocolate.

"This is Alfie and Amber Owens," she said. She motioned toward chairs, took a seat at the far end of the table, and sat quietly, her hands in her lap.

King leaned against the fridge while Hank pulled back a chair and sat forward, resting his arms on the table. He looked at the girl, then the boy. "I'm Detective Corning," he said. "And this is Detective King."

The boy glanced at King, then back at Hank, his eyes widening. "Real live detectives?"

Hank chuckled. "As real as they get."

"Are we in any trouble?" the girl asked in a low voice, her brown eyes narrowed.

"Of course not," Hank said. "In fact, we want to thank you for waiting to talk to us."

"You're welcome."

"Did you see the dead guy?" Alfie asked.

"Yes, we saw him," Hank said. "And I only have a couple questions for you."

"Fire away."

"Did you touch the ... man, or move anything around him?"

The boy frowned.

"Alfie touched him," Amber said.

Hank's head whipped toward the boy. "Did you move him?"

Alfie swatted Amber on the arm. "I only touched his foot with a stick. That's all."

"That's the truth," Amber said, pulling her arm back and frowning at her brother. "I saw him."

Hank suppressed a smile. "That's okay. It's always better never to touch anything and call the police right away. That helps us a lot."

"I was a-scared," Amber said.

Alfie straightened and pushed back his shoulders. "She's just a girl," he said. "They get scared real easy."

Hank nodded as if he understood and then looked at Amber. "It's okay to be frightened." He screwed up his face. "I get scared sometimes too."

Amber giggled, raised her chin, and gave Alfie a tight smile.

King shook his head, rolled his eyes, and went back outside.

Hank removed a notepad and pen from his inner pocket. "I need your mom's name and phone number in case I have to talk to you again."

He wrote down the information Alfie dictated, and Amber confirmed it was the truth. He turned to the woman. "I assume you didn't touch anything at the scene?"

"Land sakes, no," the woman said. "We came straight here and called the police."

Hank nodded and flipped his pad closed. "That's all I need." He put the pad away and pulled out two business cards, handing one to the woman and one to Amber. "Give this to your mom." He pointed to his phone number. "She can call me here anytime if she has any questions."

Amber took the card, tucked it into the pocket of her jeans, and gave the detective a wide smile.

Hank stood, nodded at Alfie, and winked at Amber. "Thanks, guys." He went back outside and joined King. "Let's go," he said. "That's all we're gonna get from here."

CHAPTER 29

ANNIE WAS IN the office when the doorbell rang. She peeked through the front window, saw Hank's car parked at the curb, and went to the front door.

"I came to pick up the recording of Michael Norton," Hank said when Annie opened the door.

She motioned for him to come in. He stepped inside, followed Annie into the living room, and took a seat on the couch. Annie went to the office, retrieved the recording, and brought it out to him.

Jake came into the room and sat on the other end of the couch, his feet resting on the coffee table.

Hank cleared his throat and spoke. "I think I should let you know, Michael Norton's body was found."

Annie's mouth dropped open and she stared at Hank in disbelief. "I just talked to him." She moved to the armchair, sat down, and leaned forward, waiting for Hank to continue.

"He was killed shortly after he called you," Hank said. "I just came from there, dropped King off at the precinct, and I'm on my way to see Tammy Norton now. But I wanted to listen to this recording first."

"What happened? Where was the body found?" Jake asked.

"Down by the railroad tracks near an access road. It appears he was shot elsewhere and then dumped there."

"He was afraid for his life," Annie said. "That's why he called me."

Hank stood. "Maybe we'd better play the recording. I'd like to hear it before I visit Mrs. Norton."

Annie stood and led the way to the office. She took a seat and started the recording. Jake stood by the desk while Hank sat and listened silently.

"The final known words of Michael Norton," Hank said when it was finished playing. "And he's accusing Rocky Shaft of his murder."

"Is he right about the possibility of planted evidence?" Jake asked.

"It's possible," Hank said. "And it wouldn't be the first time someone was framed. His point about the shell casing with his print on it is logical. The idea Shaft borrowed his car is a little harder to swallow, but not impossible."

"He certainly predicted his own death accurately," Annie said.

"But he's wrong about one thing," Hank interrupted.

"What's that?"

"The case doesn't get closed by his death, as he said. As

long as we have evidence pointing elsewhere, we'll continue to investigate."

"True enough," Jake said. "But would you have that evidence without this recording?"

Hank pursed his lips and said thoughtfully, "Perhaps not. All the evidence for Werner Shaft's murder points toward Norton. However, once we find Norton's killer, that evidence might point elsewhere."

"Toward Rocky Shaft, possibly."

"Perhaps," Hank said, a deep frown on his brow. "But there's even more evidence against Norton now. He had a thirty-eight-caliber gun on him, the same caliber that killed Werner Shaft. Ballistics will tell whether or not it's the same gun."

"If Rocky Shaft killed Norton, then he could've planted it."

"True enough," Hank said. "But if the crown is convinced of Norton's guilt, they can't prosecute a dead man, and the real killer might go free."

"Then we have to find out who killed Norton," Annie said.

"Norton also wore a red plaid shirt," Hank said. "The witness to Shaft's murder stated that's what the killer wore. Granted, that's only circumstantial evidence, but it's one more piece."

"What about Punky Brown or whatever his name is?" Jake asked. "Could he have had a hand in either one of these killings?"

Hank shook his head. "He has a solid alibi for Shaft's

murder. He was with his parole officer. And he was in our custody when Norton was killed."

"What about that drug money heist the three of them were involved in?" Annie asked. "Maybe they were found out and they're being picked off one by one."

"There's a problem with that theory," Jake put in. "Why would they frame Norton?"

Hank nodded. "It seems like a lot of trouble for no good reason. And it would be hard for them to set up a frame. They would need access to Norton's gun to place his fingerprints at the scene. And what about the car, and the plaid shirt? It seems to me, if it were the drug dealers getting their revenge, they would need to know a lot about Norton to set up such a solid frame job."

"So, we're back to Rocky Shaft then," Annie said.

"We certainly have to check him out a lot closer."

"The real killer—or killers—might be someone else entirely," Jake added.

"That's the thing," Hank said. "We don't know for sure if we're looking for one killer, or two."

"Michael Norton claimed his wife knew nothing about the heist," Annie said. "And Maria Shaft claimed not to know of any relationship between her husband and Norton. Hank, how true do you think that is?"

Hank shrugged. "I see no evidence against that, but it's a hard thing to prove." He paused. "But I'm not making any assumptions either way."

"I'm thinking out loud here," Jake said, "but if Norton killed Shaft, then was Norton killed out of revenge? Or did one person kill both?"

Annie said, "If it was one person, why go to the trouble of framing Norton, just to kill him?"

"To throw suspicion away from the real killer," Hank said.

"Then why kill Norton? Why not leave the frame in place? By killing Norton, it keeps a case open that otherwise could've been closed."

Hank leaned his head back, closed his eyes, and let out a long breath. "We're missing something here for sure. A lot of this doesn't make sense, and I can't come up with a clear motive for either murder."

"It might come straight back to money," Jake said. "I'd say it has something to do with the money from the heist. I don't see any other motive."

"If so," Hank said, "either Rocky Shaft is a person of interest, or his life's in danger too."

Annie stood and paced the floor. Something didn't make sense with all of this. She stopped and turned to Hank. "If the killer was convinced he had a solid frame in place, why try to kill us?"

"Because he was afraid we might prove otherwise," Jake said.

Annie nodded. "Maria Shaft hired us. Rocky Shaft knew all about that, and it might've given him a reason to get rid of us. If he framed Norton, he wouldn't want us digging into anything."

"Sure, that's possible," Hank said. "But is Rocky Shaft stupid enough to threaten Norton, and then go out and kill him?"

Annie laughed out loud and covered her mouth. "Pardon

me for laughing. I know there's nothing funny about this, but it seems we're going around in circles."

"The forensic report might give us a lead to follow," Hank said. "And when I hear from the ME, perhaps she might have something enlightening."

"I hope so," Annie said. "And I'll give it some more thought. We're missing a piece of the puzzle."

Hank stood and looked at his watch. "I'd better go see Tammy Norton now."

CHAPTER 30

Wednesday, 5:11 p.m.

HANK PULLED TO THE curb in front of the Norton house and shut off his vehicle. He wasn't looking forward to the next few minutes. This was the part of his job he dreaded the most; notifying family members was always difficult and awkward, and it never got easier with practice.

He got out of his vehicle, passed Tammy's Ford Probe parked in the driveway, and made his way up the path to the front door. He paused a moment, his finger on the doorbell, took a few quick breaths, and rang the bell.

Tammy Norton recognized him when she answered the door. "Good evening, Detective Corning," she said, a questioning look on her face.

"May I come in for a moment?" Hank asked.

Tammy stepped aside and motioned him in. Hank took an uneasy step forward and looked toward the front room. "May we sit down?"

She led him in and waved a hand toward the couch. He waited until she sat in a matching chair before he took a seat.

Hank leaned forward, fidgeted with his hands, and cleared his throat. "Mrs. Norton ..." he began and hesitated.

She tilted her head slightly to one side. "Yes?"

"I'm sorry I have to inform you, we found your husband's body this afternoon."

Tammy's eyes widened and she stared at Hank, unblinking. Then a frown took over her brow. "Are you sure it was him?"

"We're sure," Hank said. "We identified him from a photo. He was carrying his wallet as well."

Tammy was silent a moment, the frown remaining. Then she spoke, her voice quivering. "How ... how did it happen? When?"

"I'm afraid he was murdered, Mrs. Norton."

She took a sharp breath. "Murdered?"

Hank nodded. "The medical examiner estimated the time of death as a few hours ago. She'll have a more accurate time later."

Tammy closed her eyes and dropped her head back. She took a couple of deep breaths before opening her eyes again and looking at Hank.

Then the tears came, and she wiped her eyes with the palms of her hands. Then more tears.

Hank had spied a box of tissues on a stand at the end of the couch when he came in. He was in the habit of keeping an eye out for them at a time like this. They always came in handy. He stood and picked up the box, then leaned forward and offered it to Tammy.

She took a tissue, dabbed at her eyes, and then blew her nose lightly. "Do you know who … killed him?" she asked, looking at Hank through reddening eyes.

"Not yet, but we'll do our best to find out."

She nodded and closed her eyes, forcing out more tears. She blotted them away.

Hank asked softly, "Mrs. Norton, would you have any idea who might've done this?"

She shook her head. "No idea." Then she frowned and added quickly, "Maybe Rocky Shaft?"

"Why do you say that?"

"I saw him on the news. He blames my husband for his brother's murder, and he said he'd kill Michael if he got ahold of him."

"We're looking into Rocky Shaft," Hank asked. "Is there anyone else you can think of?"

She bit her lip and looked toward the ceiling a moment. "I can't think of anyone. My husband stayed out of trouble after he was released, and he worked hard. Everyone liked him, and he got along with his coworkers as far as I know."

Hank looked closely at Mrs. Norton's face. He saw the bruises Annie had mentioned, one by her left eye, and one on her chin. She didn't appear to be taking pains to cover them, her secret now exposed. He decided not to mention it to the grieving widow; it might make her defensive and cause her undue pain.

Tammy narrowed her eyes. "Detective, I hope you're convinced now my husband didn't kill Werner Shaft." She rocked back and forth in her chair, wringing her hands. "I told you yesterday, my husband's life might be in danger." Her voice held an accusing tone.

"I understand," Hank said. "And we did everything we could to find your husband." He sighed. "But we couldn't protect him if we couldn't find him."

Tammy sat up straight. "If you could have proven his innocence, he would've come forward, and he wouldn't be dead now."

Hank sat back and nodded slowly. "We did all we could, Mrs. Norton. I'm sorry about your husband. I truly am."

"Then find out who did this. Find out who killed my husband." Tammy's voice had a hint of anger in it. "He's dead and can't defend himself, so it's up to you."

Hank took a couple of slow breaths. "I'll do all I can to get at the full truth. You're going to have to trust me on that."

Her face softened and she dropped her head, sobbing. Through short, quick breaths, she managed to say, "I'm sorry, Detective. I know it's not your fault."

Hank remained quiet. He was used to taking the blame on occasion and didn't take it personally. It was all part of the grieving process.

But he couldn't rule out Norton as a murderer yet. Norton had been killed long after Shaft, and he had motive, means, and opportunity—not to mention the mountain of evidence against him.

The sobs subsided and Hank asked, "Mrs. Norton, did your husband contact you in any way since Monday?"

The pain in her eyes seemed to grow more intense. "He went to work as usual and that was the last I saw him."

"He never called you?"

"No."

Hank considered telling her about her husband's phone call to Annie and then decided it would serve no purpose. It would have to come out eventually, but now wasn't the time.

Tammy raised her head, took a shaky breath, and asked, "How was my husband killed?"

"He was shot. Once in the heart. He would've died immediately and not suffered."

She nodded almost imperceptibly, the tears welling up again. "Where ... where did you find him?"

"Down by the railway tracks. Investigators are still processing the scene, but it appears he was killed elsewhere and then taken down an access road and left near the tracks."

"Dumped like a piece of garbage," Tammy said, her lower lip quivering.

"It appears that way." Hank fidgeted uncomfortably. "They've taken him to the city morgue."

Tammy focused her pain-filled eyes on Hank. "They won't have to perform an autopsy, will they? I'd hate to think of my husband ..." Her voice trailed off and she took a deep breath before continuing. "I don't want my husband to go through that."

"It might not be necessary. The clear cause of death was a gunshot wound, but I'm afraid I can't guarantee you there won't be an autopsy. That'll be up to the medical examiner to determine."

"I don't know what good it'll do, but if it will help find Michael's killer, then ..."

"I'll see what I can do. I'll talk to the ME about that. In the meantime, you'll need to identify the body," Hank said, and added quickly, "There's no doubt it's him. It's just a formality."

Tammy nodded. "I need to see him again." She wiped away a tear. "I'm having a hard time accepting this. I guess seeing him will help."

"I'll contact you as soon as the body's ready," Hank said as he stood. "In the meantime, I'm giving this my full attention. I'll be sure to let you know anything we find out."

Tammy stood. "Thank you, Detective. Please find my husband's killer and prove his innocence."

"I'll do all I can," Hank assured her. He made his way to the front door, let himself out, and Mrs. Norton closed the door behind him.

He was glad the most uncomfortable part was over, but now he had to find a killer—or two.

CHAPTER 31

Wednesday, 5:43 p.m.

ANNIE HAD LISTENED to the phone call from Michael Norton again and was going over her notes. Norton's murder put a whole new slant on the case, and she hoped looking at things from a different angle would reveal the missing pieces of the puzzle.

The doorbell rang and she sat back, working a crick from her neck before stepping into the living room. Jake and Matty had been here a moment ago but had suddenly disappeared.

She went to the door and pulled it open. Now she knew why Jake had mysteriously vanished. He must've spied the caller through the living room window, and he and Matty would likely now be found holed up in the garage, fixing something that didn't need fixing.

The woman who stood outside looked a lot like Annie— the same midlength blond hair, blue eyes, and slim figure. But she was somewhat older, and the sour look permanently imprinted on her face camouflaged her once-attractive features.

"Hello, Mother," Annie said. "What brings you here?"

"Are you going to let me in?" Alma Roderick asked.

Annie stepped back and her mother bustled into the foyer, leaned in for an air kiss, and then strode to the kitchen. Annie followed.

"I'm on my way home from work, dear. I wanted to see if you were all right." Alma took a seat at the kitchen table.

"You could've called," Annie said.

Alma ignored the snide comment as she cast a probing gaze around the room. Finding nothing out of place, her eyes rested on her daughter. "And where's my grandson?"

Annie took a guess. "He's in the garage with Jake. They had to fix something that was uh … broken."

Alma sniffed and her voice turned to one of concern. "I do hope everything is all right between the two of you. I know you're both gone all hours of the day and night. This crazy job of yours can put a strain on any marriage." She gave Annie a know-it-all look. "I hope you aren't neglecting Matty? A child needs his mother."

"A child needs his father as well," Annie said flatly. "And Matty's with Jake now." Annie wanted to roll her eyes and shake her head, but her mother's piercing gaze stopped her. Instead she smiled as pleasantly as she could and asked, "Would you like a cup of coffee, Mother?"

"Goodness, no. I can't stay long. Your father will be home soon and he'll be wanting something to eat."

That was good news. A few minutes with her mother would be enough to last a week.

Annie racked her brain for something to say. Finally, "How are things at work?"

"Not so bad now that I'm there. Goodness, before I started, the place was in such a shambles. People coming without appointments, others not showing up when they should." She shook her head, her lips in a straight line. "I don't know how they ever stayed in business."

Annie smiled. She knew the hair salon where her mother worked part-time was a thriving business many years before her mother started, and would likely be there many years after she was gone.

The doorbell rang again and Annie hoped it was the men in white coats coming for her mother.

No such luck. When she opened the door, a microphone was pushed at her and the voice of Lisa Krunk asked, "Mrs. Lincoln, I wonder if I may ask you a few questions?"

Annie hesitated and looked at Don, standing beside Lisa, holding the camera, its red light already glowing. She knew anything she said, even a refusal, was liable to be on the news, so she forced a smile and said, "I have a few minutes."

She glanced toward the kitchen. It would be best to keep her mother unaware of this, so she stepped outside, closed the door quietly, and looked at Lisa.

Lisa smiled tightly. "Mrs. Lincoln, I understand you and your husband are investigating the murder of Werner Shaft. Can you tell me about any progress you might've made?"

Annie thought quickly. The truth was, as far as she was concerned, they hadn't made any progress yet. "This case is still ongoing, and though there are persons of interest, there's no solid suspect at this point."

Lisa continued, "I understand Michael Norton was found dead. He was a suspect in the case, and now with his murder, are you looking elsewhere? And do you have a suspect in his murder?"

Annie knew Lisa had people everywhere, and wasn't surprised the reporter had found out about Norton so quickly. "I don't have anything to add. The police are looking into Michael Norton's death, and it might be better to direct your questions to them."

"What about the attempts on the lives of you and your husband, Mrs. Lincoln?"

"The man who attempted to harm my husband and me has been apprehended."

From the corner of her eye, Annie saw the door open. She turned her head to see her mother standing in the doorway, her hands on her hips, a deep frown on her face.

A hint of a smile appeared on Lisa's lips and she swung the microphone toward Alma. Lisa and Annie's mother had met in the past, and there was no affection between the two of them.

"Mrs. Roderick," Lisa said. "Has there been any attempt on your life, or do you feel this has put you in any danger?"

Alma raised her chin. "My daughter has a dangerous job and she does it well. When people like you come around, it can only result in making things worse. Of course we're all in danger. Why, only a few weeks ago, I was confronted—"

Annie put her hand over the mike and stepped between Lisa and her mother. "Lisa, I'm trusting you that anything my mother says is strictly off the record. I don't mind giving you a short interview from time to time, but please keep my family out of it."

Lisa narrowed her eyes as if considering that. Then she nodded curtly. "Fair enough."

Annie removed her hand from the mike. "As I said, the police have not made an arrest in the murder of either Werner Shaft or Michael Norton. It's still an ongoing investigation, and there's nothing else I can tell you at the moment."

Alma backed from the doorway and the door slammed behind her, making Annie jump.

"Thank you, Mrs. Lincoln," Lisa said, forcing a smile. She signaled to Don and the red light blinked off.

Annie stepped back in the house as Lisa and Don turned and made their way back to the Channel 7 News van.

"You shouldn't talk to those people," Alma said, when Annie returned to the kitchen. "You don't need to get your face out there for every crazy to see." She moved into the hallway. "I must go now. Please be more careful."

Annie watched her mother march out the front door, then shook her head and went to the garage. Jake sat on a wooden box, fiddling with something that appeared to have come from a car engine. Matty stood beside him. They looked up when Annie entered.

"You guys can come out of here now," she said. "The danger is past."

CHAPTER 32

Wednesday, 7:05 p.m.

HANK FELT WEARY. It had been a long day following a late night the evening before, and combined with the emotional events of the day, he was ready for a long rest.

But his mind wouldn't quit. He ran the facts of the case over and over in his head, trying to devise a working scenario he could run with, but nothing seemed to fit.

His desk was littered with folders, printouts, and reports, each one holding pieces of the puzzle he couldn't bring together into something cohesive.

He plugged the flash drive Annie had given him into his computer and listened intently to her conversation with Michael Norton. The caller put the blame for the murder of Werner Shaft squarely on the shoulders of Rocky Shaft.

Other than that accusation, the only thing pointing to Rocky was his threat to kill Norton. It was reason enough to question him further, but unless an interview revealed something incriminating, he had no reason to hold him.

Hank dug through the stack of folders, pulled out the report on Rocky Shaft, and flipped it open. Shaft had a record for an assault that had taken place many years ago. He had served thirty days, been released, and stayed clean since. That offense, combined with the threat on Norton, could mean he had an anger problem.

It could also mean Shaft's threat was due to the grief of his brother's death. Any good lawyer would argue that.

Hank sat back and closed his eyes. If Rocky and Werner Shaft, along with Norton, were involved in the drug money heist Norton had mentioned, and the dealers were out for revenge, that could explain everything—except the evidence against Norton for Shaft's murder.

He opened his eyes, leaned forward, and made a note to get King to check on any heist that might've taken place in the drug world a few months ago.

He looked at his watch, picked up the phone, and called Rocky Shaft. Shaft had just gotten home from work, and though at first he balked at a visit from Hank, he gave in and agreed to an interview. Hank didn't see the need to bring him in to the station. He wasn't going to arrest him. Besides, Hank might have a few questions for Maria Shaft as well.

Detective King had left for home some time ago. Hank didn't care to have him in on this interview, anyway. He wanted to keep it civil, and King had a way of putting people on edge at the wrong time.

He swept together the reports and folders, tucked them into his briefcase, and left the quiet precinct.

When Hank arrived at the Shaft residence, Maria's dark green Mazda wasn't there. The only vehicle in the driveway was a red Ford pickup. Rocky had been at work the last time Hank had visited, but from the printouts, he knew the vehicle was Rocky's.

Hank parked at the curb, grabbed his briefcase from the passenger seat, got out, and went to the pickup. There was a tarp in the back, neatly folded. There wasn't much else there. A spare tire, a length of nylon rope, a red metal toolbox. Hank wanted to lift the lid, but that would constitute an illegal search. He wondered if the box held more than screwdrivers, wrenches, or pliers.

He turned, strode up the pathway, and rang the bell. Rocky Shaft answered the door after the second ring, stepped back, and beckoned him in.

"What's this all about?" Shaft asked after they took a seat in the front room. "Did you find my brother's killer?"

Hank snapped open his briefcase and laid it on the couch beside him. He looked at Shaft. "I'm afraid I have nothing conclusive to report, Mr. Shaft. We're still looking into the evidence, but I have a few questions for you."

Shaft sat back, frowned, and crossed his legs. "Fire away. And call me Rocky."

"Rocky, this afternoon Michael Norton's body was found. He was murdered." Hank eyed the man closely, watching for his reaction.

Rocky's eyes shot open and he stared at Hank, unblinking. "I hope you don't think I had anything to do with that?" he asked at last, his eyes narrowing.

"You threatened to kill him," Hank said.

Rocky sighed. "Yes, I did." He uncrossed his legs and leaned forward. "I was angry because I think he killed my brother. But I didn't mean it."

"Perhaps not," was all Hank said. He reached into his briefcase, removed a folder, and flipped it open. "Mr. Shaft ... Rocky, on the evening of your brother's murder, you left work at seven. Where did you go after that?"

"I came straight home."

"And yet, when I called that evening, no one answered the phone."

"I live in the basement apartment. I was down there and I wouldn't have heard the telephone."

"Were you alone all evening?"

"Yes, I was." Rocky frowned. "Do you think I had something to do with my brother's death?"

"I'm trying to fill in the blanks," Hank said. He flipped over a page in the folder, studied it a moment, and asked, "Where were you today between the hours of twelve noon and three p.m.?"

"I was at work." Rocky paused. "I went out for lunch at twelve thirty and was back by one thirty."

Hank pulled out a pen and made a note. "Where did you go?"

"Marcy's Deli. Down the street from where I work at Richmond Distributing."

Hank made another note. "Did anyone see you there?"

Rocky shrugged one shoulder and sat back. "It's a busy place. I have no idea."

"Do you have a receipt for the meal?"

Rocky's face darkened and he spoke sharply. "I don't keep the receipts."

Hank nodded, made a note, and flipped another page. "Do you own a gun, Rocky?"

Rocky's nostrils flared. "No."

Now for the big question. "What can you tell me about the drug money heist you were involved in a few months ago?"

Rocky seemed genuinely bewildered. "What are you talking about?"

Hank waved the paper. "According to this, you, Werner, and Michael Norton heisted some money from drug dealers."

Rocky exploded from the chair. "I don't know where you got that information, and I have no idea what you're talking about. I was never involved in anything like that."

"Relax, Mr. Shaft," Hank said, waving toward the chair. "Sit down, please."

Rocky folded his arms, his face reddening. "I don't have to sit down. This interview is going nowhere, and you're accusing me of things I had nothing to do with."

Hank looked up at the angry man and spoke calmly. "I'm not accusing you. I'm asking about allegations others have made."

"Do I need a lawyer?" Rocky asked, his thick brows in a tight line.

"Not unless you're guilty of something."

"The only thing I'm guilty of is trying to find out who killed my brother." Rocky's voice became shrill. "I don't care who killed Norton. Frankly, I'm glad he's dead, because I think he killed my brother, and you're wasting my time." He pointed toward the foyer. "This interview is over. Please leave."

Hank packed up his briefcase, snapped it shut, and stood. "Thank you for your time, Mr. Shaft. I'll be in touch with any developments."

The door slammed behind Hank as he left the house. He wasn't sure what he'd gotten from this interview, but one thing was certain: Rocky Shaft was a very angry man.

CHAPTER 33

DAY 4 - Thursday, 8:45 a.m.

ANNIE HAD HOPED a good night's sleep would clear her mind and allow her to come up with something new, but after bustling Matty off to school and finishing her second cup of coffee, all she could do was sit at her desk and stare at her notes.

Jake wasn't much help, either. He had wandered around the house like he was lost before heading downstairs for his morning workout. Annie could tell his mind was busy, and when he came into the office and slouched back in a chair, she knew he had drawn a blank.

She asked him anyway, "Come up with anything?"

"Nope."

Annie sat back. "Usually there's a clear-cut motive—somebody benefits from another's death—but I'm not seeing anything this time."

"If it's about the drug money, and Rocky Shaft is out to get it, he's going to be careful for a while."

Annie steepled her fingers, looked at Jake over top, and mused, "I wonder where they're keeping the money."

"Could be anywhere. In a locker. Under somebody's floorboards. Not likely in a bank account."

"If Rocky Shaft is the killer, he knows."

"He's not gonna go near it," Jake said. "Especially if his accomplices are dead. He knows it's safe."

"Perhaps," Annie said. "But if he's as greedy as Norton suggested, he might not be able to keep his hands off it."

"You might be right, but he'd have a hard time spending any of it. They're watching him too closely."

"There's still a possibility of an affair going on between Maria and Rocky Shaft."

"Sure," Jake said. "But why kill Norton?"

"Because he found out about it?"

Jake drew his legs in and leaned forward. "So Rocky kills his brother, frames Norton, and then kills Norton too? Doesn't sound logical. By killing Norton, it leaves an unsolved murder, and puts Rocky in the spotlight."

Annie blew out a breath and shook her head in frustration. "You're right. Doesn't make sense."

Jake frowned. "Here's another crazy scenario. Do you think it's possible we're looking at two separate and unrelated murders?"

Annie drummed her fingers on the desktop a moment. "I don't think so. That's too much of a coincidence."

"You're probably right," Jake said and slouched back down.

"Don't feel bad," Annie said. "You're not the only one

drawing a blank. Even Hank is stumped on this one."

Jake yawned and said in an offhand manner, "Maybe we should visit the Shafts' neighbors."

"Perhaps that's not such a bad idea."

"You think so?"

"Do we have anything better to do?"

Jake stood. "I'm game."

"We'll take my car," Annie said. She stood and went to the kitchen, got her handbag and keys, and met Jake at the front door.

A few minutes later, Annie pulled her Escort to the curb in front of the Shaft house. There was an empty lot on one side and a small brick bungalow on the other, separated from the Shaft house by an evergreen hedge.

"That's our best bet," Annie said, pointing to the bungalow. She pulled the car ahead thirty feet and stopped.

"What if no one's home?" Jake asked.

"We'll soon see. There's a vehicle parked in the driveway."

The door opened to Jake's knock by an elderly man, a cane in one shaky hand, and he looked at Jake over top of a pair of reading glasses. "Yes?"

Jake introduced Annie and himself. "Could we ask you a few questions?"

The old man squinted at Jake, then offered Annie a smile. "Glad to help," he said. "Sara and I don't get a lot of visitors." He stepped back. "Come right on in. Make yourself at home, and don't mind the cat and she won't mind you."

Water could be heard running from down the hallway, probably from the kitchen.

"Sara," the man called in a shaky voice. "We got company."

The water stopped, and in a moment a woman appeared in the hallway, wiping her hands on an apron. Her gray hair was worked up into a bun, and a pleasant smile adorned her face as she shuffled toward them. She stopped and beckoned. "Bring them on into the kitchen, Abe. Where's your manners?"

A jug of orange juice and a generous plate of baked goods were set in front of them almost before the Lincolns could pull back chairs and sit down.

Sara poured the juice and pushed the plate of goodies toward Jake. "Fill up on this, young man. You look like you could hold a few. And there's plenty more where that came from."

Jake thanked her and helped himself.

"Ma'am," Annie began.

"You can call me Sara." She pointed at the old man. "And this here's Abe." She patted Annie's hand and beamed. "Sorry to interrupt, dear. You go right ahead."

Annie smiled. The woman reminded her of everyone's grandmother. "Sara, I don't know if you've heard about Werner Shaft's death, but we're looking into it."

"Dear me, what a dreadful thing that is. Yes, we heard about that. Shocking." She looked at the old man. "Wouldn't you say, Abe?"

Abe nodded. "Shocking. Indeed."

"And how can we help, my dear?" Sara asked.

"Did you know Werner Shaft?"

"Oh, sure. Werner was a fine man. Can't say as much for his brother."

"Rocky?" Jake said, popping a chocolate square into his mouth.

"Has a bad temper, I'll say that. Why, he's always after Abe about one thing or another. Isn't he, Abe?"

"Sure is."

"What about Maria? Do she and Rocky get along?"

Sara covered her mouth. "Don't know as I should gossip 'bout this, but I think them two are up to something."

"Such as?" Jake asked.

Sara leaned in and lowered her voice. "Well, they're just too close. Many's the time when they don't think anyone's watching and I see them in the backyard together."

"When Werner was there?"

"No. No. When he wasn't there."

"What did you see?" Jake asked. He took a chug of orange juice.

"Don't know as I should say," the old woman said.

"Go ahead, Sara," Abe said. "You ain't never kept nothing quiet for long anyway. Might as well spill the beans on this one."

Sara whispered, "They get amorous."

Annie tilted her head slightly to one side. "An affair?"

"Sure as tarnation."

Jake and Annie exchanged a look. She knew he was thinking the same as she was. Could Rocky or Maria have killed Werner? Or perhaps they were in it together?

Annie eyed Sara closely. "You're sure about this?"

Sara sat back and looked at Abe. "Tell them, Abe. You've seen them carrying on."

Abe nodded. "I have to confirm what the old woman says. There's something up between them two and it ain't innocent."

Annie pulled a business card from her handbag and slid it in front of Sara. "You've been a big help. Call me if you can think of anything else."

"I sure will," Sara said. "You can bet I'm gonna be keepin' a sharp eye out from now on."

Abe chuckled. "I can vouch for that. It's what she does best."

Annie and Jake stood and thanked them again, and Sara saw them to the door. "Drop in again some time," the old woman said as they left.

Annie laughed and glanced at Jake when the door closed behind them. "Maybe we should offer Sara a part-time job. She's got the knack."

Jake chuckled. "She'd probably be good at stakeouts."

They got in the car and Annie started the engine, then turned to Jake. "The affair between Rocky and Maria could explain a lot. The problem is, it doesn't tell us anything about why Michael Norton was killed."

"Did Rocky kill his brother and frame Norton for it?"

"It's possible," Annie said. "But then we're back to the same question. Who killed Norton, and why?"

CHAPTER 34

Thursday, 9:22 a.m.

AS TIRED AS HANK had been the night before, he was robbed of sleep by the perplexing facts of the case running through his mind. He'd risen early to get a fresh start, and though he'd been up for a couple of hours, he felt he was making little headway.

A call to King to see if the detective had found any information on the drug heist went unanswered. A quick study of his notes revealed nothing new, and to make matters worse, a plugged sink in the bathroom wasted a half hour of valuable time.

He downed a quick breakfast, made a short phone call to Amelia over coffee, and was raring to go.

He gathered up the stacks of notes, reports, and folders and stuffed them into his briefcase. After fastening his service weapon in place, he headed out the door, determined to make the day count.

His old Chevy clanked and banged when he turned the key. It had served him faithfully for several years, but by the sounds of the engine, he would need a new vehicle before long. Not an easy thing to do with only a cop's salary and the small car allowance RHPD allowed him.

When he arrived at the precinct, he parked behind it, noticed King's car wasn't there, and hoped the detective was doing something productive for a change.

The precinct was in high gear when Hank stepped inside. Cops leaned over their desks, or consulted with one another. Captain Diego's face was buried in paperwork, and across the room, Callaway squinted at his monitor.

The heat of the day was already infiltrating the room, the useless air conditioner doing little except rumble, and Hank made a mental note to talk to Diego about replacing the worn-out piece of junk.

He headed for the break room. This was starting to be a bad day. Someone had drained the coffee pot and left it turned on. Hank started a fresh pot. At least he knew it would be palatable, not like most of the rotgut sludge he had to endure when someone else made it.

Things took a turn for the better when he got to his desk, set his coffee down, and spied the medical examiner's report regarding the murder of Michael Norton sitting dead center on his desk. Beside it lay the preliminary ballistics report. He sat and pulled up his chair, booted up his computer, and flipped open the folder containing the ME's findings.

The listed cause of death was not surprising—a gunshot wound causing exsanguination. Norton had bled to death after catastrophic injury to the heart.

The manner of death was homicide—that was obvious, and Nancy concluded Norton had been killed elsewhere, perhaps a half hour prior to being dumped near the railroad tracks.

The interesting part was the trajectory of the bullet. Gunshot residue indicated it had been fired from a distance of eighteen to twenty-four inches and entered the body at a thirty-degree downward angle.

Hank did some quick calculations, and as far as he could tell, the victim had been either standing or kneeling when shot. Norton might've been tied to a chair, or on his knees, begging for his life when the fatal bullet had entered his body.

An examination of the back of the victim's shirt revealed small nicks and tears with ground-in dirt, consistent with the body being dragged a distance. To Hank, that meant Norton had been transported there in a vehicle, then dragged across the ground and deposited by the bushes. There was no other explanation he could see.

There were also lesions on the arms, face, and hands—nicks, bruises, and abrasions, probably defensive wounds, or at the least, an indication of a struggle.

Norton had fought and begged for his life, and he had lost.

Blood alcohol levels, as well as blood and urine drug screens, were normal.

He closed the folder. Nothing else in the report revealed anything unusual, but he would go over it again later.

The ballistics report revealed exactly what Hank had expected. The weapon Norton had carried was the same one that had fired the fatal bullet into Werner Shaft.

The bullet lodged in Norton's heart was also .38 caliber, fired from a different weapon than the one found on the body. The ballistics ID system returned a negative. It was another unregistered weapon, never before used in a shooting as far as the system could tell.

That was all Jameson had for him at the moment. Hank hoped to see the rest of the findings later in the day. He was especially interested in the possibility of tire tracks and any trace evidence recovered from the scene. With the lack of surveillance cameras anywhere in the area, and no witnesses to be found, he hoped for something solid from forensics.

Hank looked up as Callaway approached his desk and handed him a sheet of paper. "I got the bank records on Rocky Shaft you requested. There's an interesting withdrawal."

"Thanks, Callaway."

Hank took the paper and glanced at it. Callaway had highlighted a withdrawal for six thousand dollars cash from Shaft's bank account on Tuesday morning. Could that be to pay off the hitman? Punky Brown had never been paid, but Brown had indicated the fee for his services was five thousand. More circumstantial evidence? Perhaps. But what was the extra thousand for?

"Anything else you need, Hank?"

Hank looked up at the young cop. "Not right now. I'm sure there'll be something later."

Callaway returned to his desk as the precinct doors swung open and Detective King swaggered in. The grin on his face revealed he had something to share. He waved a finger at

Hank, strode to the break room, took his sweet time about making a coffee, and then approached Hank's desk.

Hank sat back and watched patiently as King settled into a chair and stretched out, one sneakered foot resting on the corner of the desk. King hadn't shaved again this morning. He always managed to have three days' growth on his face, even after he shaved. It was a mystery even Hank couldn't solve.

King sipped at his coffee. Hank waited some more.

"Harland Eastwood," King said at last.

King had a way of dropping names as if making a big reveal, and then waiting for a response before explaining.

Hank took the bait. "Who's Harland Eastwood?"

King took another sip and set his cup on the desk. "One of the druggies robbed by Shaft and his friends."

Hank sat forward and rested his arms on the desk. "Does Eastwood know who robbed them?"

"I haven't talked to him yet," King said. "I got the name from a CI. Had to get him out of bed."

Hank sighed lightly, shuffled the papers on his desk, and remained patient.

King continued, "Seems like all these criminal types sleep until noon. Guess that's what happens when you're up half the night."

"Does your informant know where to find Eastwood?"

King pulled a scrap of paper from his shirt pocket and waved it. "Got the address." He handed it to Hank.

"Rough part of town," Hank said, after looking at the paper. "You'd think if they were big-time drug dealers they could afford to live in a better place."

"Apparently, Eastwood is a flunky. Not one of the big shots. Does deliveries, pickups, that sort of thing."

Hank frowned. "That's the best you could get? A flunky?"

"He might not be top brass, but if he knows anything, it's gonna be easier to get something from him."

Hank swept the reports into a pile, dropped them into his briefcase, and stood. "Let's go see if we can find this Eastwood character."

CHAPTER 35

Thursday, 10:24 a.m.

JAKE WAS STRETCHED out on the couch, a cushion under his head, his hands tucked behind it. The television was on and muted, but Jake wasn't watching it. He stared at the ceiling, sorting through the facts, devising a workable plan of attack.

Though Rocky Shaft appeared to be the obvious suspect for Norton's murder, Jake wasn't so sure. However, the revelation by Shaft's neighbors regarding a possible affair was foremost in his mind.

It seemed to Jake, other than the affair, Shaft was trying to hide something and money played a big part in it.

He swung his legs to the floor, stood, and went into the office. Annie was typing furiously at the keyboard, and when he entered, she stopped and looked over at him.

He approached the desk and perched on the corner. "I thought I might go see Rocky Shaft," he said.

"That suits me fine. I got the cell phone number of one of Michael Norton's neighbors from Hank, and I have an appointment to visit her at her work at noon, during her lunch break."

"Great. Then I'll see you back here this afternoon. I'll call you if I come up with anything interesting." Jake gave her a quick peck on the lips and left the office.

He unplugged his cell phone from the charger, slipped it into a holder on his belt, and grabbed his car keys from a hook by the door on the way out.

The Firebird purred like a tiger under control when he turned the key. He looked at his watch; Shaft should be at work, and if not, Jake wanted to know why.

Richmond Distributing sat on a couple of acres surrounded by a chain-link fence. A pair of warehouses occupied much of that space, the rest taken up by parking areas, tractor-trailers, and shipping containers.

From the information he'd gleaned online, Jake knew the company did local and national distribution for a number of organizations, as well as drop-shipping services for a variety of mail-order and online firms.

Driving onto the property was not much different from going to the mall. There was no gate, no security, and the public was always welcome to visit the showroom displaying a range of items for retail purchase.

Jake parked in one of the guest spots, grabbed an official-looking baseball cap from the backseat, and walked around behind the largest building to the shipping doors at the rear.

A row of vehicles was parked along the back fence, and

Jake spied a red Ford pickup. That would be Shaft's vehicle. He wandered over and checked the license plate to be sure. It was Shaft's. He would be in the building somewhere.

A trailer was backed up to the loading dock, and the hum of a lift truck could be heard as it unloaded skids of merchandise to be redistributed. An access door beside the dock was propped open by a concrete block, and from where Jake stood, workers could be seen engrossed in their tasks.

He stepped inside and looked around. No one paid him any attention; perhaps they assumed he was a truck or local delivery van driver.

Jake didn't know where he would find Shaft. He only knew he worked in the shipping department. Half of the enormous room was filled with rows and rows of shelving, skids piled three layers high, and mounds of shipping material. Shaft could be anywhere.

The entire right wall of the building was one long counter, weigh scales and postage machines at intervals, where pickers filled orders for shipping to individuals and small companies. Shaft wasn't among those preoccupied workers.

To his left, on the far side of the loading dock, Jake spied a small office. He waited for a lift truck to rumble by, then strolled across the floor and peered into the room.

Rocky Shaft sat at a small desk, filling out some forms. He seemed to have become shipping manager in place of his brother. Certainly the promotion would not be a motive for murder, just a logical step for the company to take in light of Werner's demise.

Jake tapped on the open door. Shaft looked up and his

face darkened. He tossed his pen on the desk, spun around, and glared at the visitor. "What do you want?"

Jake disregarded the surly tone and smiled politely. "I want to talk to you about your brother."

Shaft's voice took on a calmer tone. "What about him?"

"Norton didn't kill him," Jake said.

Shaft remained quiet a moment, then said, "Norton killed my brother. I have no doubt about that, and all the evidence proves he did."

"Evidence can be planted."

Shaft shrugged. "And who planted the evidence?"

"Maybe you."

Shaft slammed a fist on a table. "Are you accusing me of killing my own brother?"

"I'm not accusing anyone," Jake said calmly. "I'll let the evidence speak for itself."

"Fine. Let the evidence speak and it'll show I had nothing to do with it. You're making accusations based on nothing."

"Not exactly nothing," Jake said. He paused and watched closely for Shaft's reaction. "Did your brother know you were having an affair with his wife?"

Shaft flew from his chair and took a step toward Jake. His left fist clenched, a finger of his other hand pointing at Jake. "I'm not having an affair, and you know it."

"According to witnesses, you are."

Shaft folded his arms. "What witnesses?"

"You can drop the pretense, Shaft," Jake said. "You might as well admit it."

Shaft pointed toward the door, his face red. "Get out of here."

"Maria admits you're having an affair," Jake said.

Shaft dropped into the chair, bewildered, frowning. He glared at Jake a moment, then said, "Just go."

Jake noted there was no second denial, just more anger. He took a chance. "I know where the money is, Shaft."

"What money?"

"From the drug heist."

A frown took over Shaft's brow and his eyes narrowed. "I don't believe you."

Jake shrugged. "You don't have to believe me. I'm only giving you a heads-up. You aren't the only one who knows where it's hidden, and certain people love to talk."

Shaft stood again, took two steps toward Jake, and stopped. "I don't have to speak to you or answer any of your questions. I've done nothing wrong." He reached forward, poked Jake in the chest, and spoke in a low, menacing tone. "Get out of here."

Jake didn't budge. "I know you killed Norton and I can prove it."

Shaft's face flushed with anger. "You have no proof because I didn't kill anyone."

"I also know Maria's in on it," Jake said. "She knows the whole story."

"Leave Maria out of this. She knows nothing about anything."

"You're quite protective of her, aren't you?" Jake said.

Shaft's nostrils flared and he jutted his chin. "Of course I am. She's my brother's wife and she wouldn't hurt a flea."

"Thanks for your time," Jake said as he turned and

stepped outside the office door. He waved a hand. "See you later, Shaft."

The door slammed behind him. Jake turned back and put his ear to the door. He could make out Shaft cursing, then a few moments later, a murmuring voice. Shaft was on the phone with someone, perhaps Maria.

Jake went back outside and nodded at a worker coming through the door. The truck was pulling away from the loading dock, another one waiting to back in.

He hurried to the front of the building, hopped in his car, and drove it around back, parking it five slots past Shaft's pickup. He jumped out, moved to the rear of the property, sat on the grassy strip along the fence, leaned back, and brought up his knees.

Though Shaft's face had told otherwise, he hadn't admitted to the affair. And if his words were any indication, he'd come close to admitting he knew about the money. Whether or not he killed Norton, Jake didn't know, but one thing he knew for sure, Rocky Shaft was involved in this somehow.

He had riled Shaft up pretty good, and if Shaft was as anxious as Jake assumed he would be, then the angry man was going to make a move, and make it soon.

CHAPTER 36

HANK TURNED the steering wheel and eased the Chevy onto Auburn Street. To the right, small houses that had been the standard for modern family homes in bygone days now stood as examples of decay, neglect, and abuse.

Across the street, decrepit tenements and graffiti-clad low-rises lined the inner-city street. According to the address King had obtained, Harland Eastwood lived in one of them.

King peered through the passenger-side window as the vehicle rolled over potholes and bulging asphalt. "Pull up here," he said, waving toward the curb. He pointed to one of the buildings. "That's the place."

Hank pulled over and shut down the engine, and they stepped out. Litter swam by his feet as a sudden breeze came up, whirling dust and debris in and out of the gutter.

A pair of lethargic women lounged in lawn chairs on a postage-stamp lawn. With nothing better to occupy their time, they watched curiously as the cops crossed the street and approached the ravaged building.

Home to the idle poor, the unemployed, and the squatters, the ancient two-story building was doomed never to see a much-needed makeover. Rather, when the booming city demanded more space, these buildings would be leveled, and gleaming new high-rises to house the middle class would take their place. The poor would be pushed out, forced to huddle elsewhere.

King pushed open the door leading into a darkened lobby. The door squealed as it scraped against the tiled floor and remained open.

"Upstairs. 204," King said, striding across the lobby to a set of concrete-and-metal steps leading upward.

Hank followed him to the second floor, where the top of the steps opened into a short hallway. A musty smell filled the close, warm air, mixed with what could be human waste or something an animal had left behind. It filled Hank's nose, and he could taste it on his tongue.

They walked the tattered and stained carpeting to the end of the hall and stopped in front of 204.

King tapped on the door. There was no answer.

He tapped again, waited a moment, and then rammed the door with his shoulder. It held.

Hank grabbed King's arm. "You can't do that. We have no probable cause, and no warrant to search this place."

King spun to face Hank. "We're not going to search. Just talk." He wrested his arm from Hank's grasp and rammed the door again. Wood splintered and crackled as it burst inward and slammed against the inner wall.

Hank was growing tired of King's cowboy attitude. He

would always have his partner's back, but Hank was determined to make it clear he wasn't going to put up with King's illegal antics much longer.

"Relax, Hank," King said as he stepped into the apartment.

If it were possible, the stench inside the room was worse than in the hallway. Human sweat, and something like the smell of rotting fish, greeted Hank as he followed King in.

His eyes roved over the contents of the one-room apartment, not much more than piles of old clothes, fifty-year-old furniture, and castoffs of all kinds.

Across the room, a man clad only in boxer shorts, a beer belly hanging over his waistline, struggled to a seating position on a caved-in couch. His dark, sleep-filled eyes were wide, and the mouth on his oval face hung open.

"What the—"

King interrupted. "Harland Eastwood?" he asked, pulling back his shirt to reveal the badge fastened to his belt.

"I didn't do nothin'," Eastwood said, brushing back his stringy dark hair.

King looked down at the startled man. "That's not what I hear. Possession of drugs with intent to traffic." King's eyes roved around the room. "I bet if I looked around a little, I'd come up with something."

"Where's your warrant?" Eastwood asked, sitting back and folding his arms.

"We have probable cause," King lied.

Hank nudged King aside and turned to Eastwood. "Look. We just want to ask you a couple questions, then we'll go. We can forget all about drug possession charges."

Eastwood's eyes narrowed. "What kind of questions?"

"About the guys you work for."

"I'm unemployed."

"Great," Hank said. "Then you won't mind talking to us about your ex-boss."

Eastwood gave a blank, confused stare.

"We want to know about a drug money heist that went down a few months ago," King said. "Talk to us and we were never here."

"Mind if I get dressed?" Eastwood asked. He leaned forward, reached down, and picked up a pair of faded jeans beside the couch, then stood and slipped them on. He pulled a wrinkled t-shirt from a pile and worked it over his head.

"What d'you wanna know?" the man asked, tucking his hands into his pockets.

"Who pulled the heist?" Hank asked.

Eastwood shrugged. "Nobody knows." He paused. "As far as I can tell, that is."

"Somebody must know."

"Maybe. But if so, they didn't tell me."

"How much money was taken?" King asked.

"About five hundred large. Least, that's what I heard."

"How many gunmen?"

Eastwood cocked his head. "You mean, how many guys robbed them?"

"Yes. How many?"

"Three."

"You're sure?" Hank asked.

"Positive. There were three."

"Because you were there, weren't you?" King asked.

Eastwood said nothing.

King reached out and pushed Eastwood onto the couch. "You were there, right?"

Eastwood looked up at King. "Maybe."

Hank touched King's arm. "It doesn't matter. All that matters is if he's telling the truth."

"It's the truth," the man said.

"Did you recognize any of them?" King asked.

Eastwood shook his head adamantly. "They wore masks."

"And your boss has no idea who it was?"

"Not that I know of." Eastwood tilted his head slightly. "Why do you guys care about this? If drug money gets stolen, why are the cops involved?"

Hank looked at King, then back at Eastwood. "Because one of the guys we think pulled the robbery is dead. Maybe two. And we want to know who killed them."

Eastwood's eyes darted back and forth between the two cops. "I hope you're not looking at me for that."

"Should we be?"

"Of course not." Eastwood swallowed hard. "And I don't think my boss was involved either or I would've heard about it."

"Don't you mean your ex-boss?" King asked.

"Yeah. That's what I meant."

"You can tell your ex-boss when you talk to him, probably as soon as we leave, if he killed anyone, we're coming for him."

Eastwood moistened his lips. "I'll … I'll tell him."

"One more question," Hank said. "Did the robbers use pistols or rifles?"

"Pistols."

"Thirty-eights?"

"Don't know."

Hank looked at King. "Anything else?"

"Yeah, maybe," King said, then looked at Eastwood. "Stay out of trouble because I might not overlook your indiscretions next time." He paused. "But you can always get ahold of me if you find out anything else. That might earn you a get-out-of-jail-free card." King pulled out a business card and flipped it onto the couch. "You can always reach me here."

Eastwood glanced at the card, then back at King. "I ain't a snitch."

"Keep the card anyway. You never know when it might come in handy," King said, then turned to Hank. "Shall we let this guy get back to his beauty sleep?"

Hank nodded, then turned and left the apartment. King followed, pulling the broken door closed behind him.

Hank whirled around, put a hand on King's chest, and pushed him against the wall. He moved in close and scowled. "You can do whatever you want on your own time, but when I'm around, we do things right. Next time, we knock. We don't go busting doors down." He paused. "Got that?"

King nodded and said dryly, "Whatever you say, Hank."

Hank narrowed his eyes, glared a moment longer, then straightened King's collar and turned away. "Let's get out of here."

CHAPTER 37

Thursday, 11:05 a.m.

JAKE SAT ON THE grass, leaning against the fence. He was half-hidden from the view of anyone who might exit the rear of the warehouse, and he waited patiently for Rocky Shaft.

If Jake's claim to know the whereabouts of the heist money made Shaft nervous at all, Jake expected him to take steps to secure it, or at the least, to ensure it was untouched.

He rolled to one side and ducked out of sight when Shaft exited the building. Jake looked at his watch. It wasn't lunchtime yet, but Shaft was headed somewhere. He had slipped away early and was walking straight toward his vehicle.

Jake stood, keeping low, and moved to his car. He stood at the driver side and watched as Shaft opened the door of his pickup.

Jake's eyes bulged as a man appeared at the back of the truck, an upraised baseball bat held firmly in both hands.

Even from where Jake stood, he saw hostility written all over the newcomer's face.

"Shaft," Jake yelled.

Too late. The man stepped forward and the bat connected with Shaft's back. Jake sprang into action as the victim went down. He heard the dull thud of the weapon striking, again and again.

Jake reached Shaft's vehicle and the man stood straight, raised the bat, and glared at Jake. Shaft moved and groaned, then lay still again, now flat on his back.

"Put it down," Jake demanded.

The attacker looked back at Shaft and gritted his teeth, striking the victim again. Shaft groaned and curled into a ball.

Jake stepped forward as the man backed up and pointed the club toward Jake. "Stay back."

"Put the bat down," Jake repeated.

The assailant swished the weapon through the air. "You're next if you don't stay back."

Jake took another step forward. "Who're you?"

The attacker pointed at Shaft. "This guy killed my cousin and I'm giving him what he deserves."

"Who's your cousin?"

"Michael Norton was my cousin." He raised the bat, clenched his jaw, and glared at Shaft.

The man on the ground held his ribs and rolled to his back. He groaned. "I ... I didn't kill Norton." The words came out amid puffs of air. "It wasn't me." He groaned again and pulled up his knees.

Jake took another step forward, stood by Shaft, and reached for the club. "Give it to me."

The man poked the tip of the bat toward Jake. Jake grabbed for it and missed, the weapon connecting with the back of his hand.

The attacker swung the bat again. Jake leaned back as it zinged past his face.

The man was average height and weight, and would be easy enough for Jake to subdue under normal circumstances, but this wasn't normal. The man held a potentially deadly weapon and Jake didn't want to feel the wrong end of it.

He held out a hand, palm up. "You've punished him enough. Give me the bat."

The assailant shook his head. Jake moved forward, stepped over Shaft, and then ducked as the weapon whistled over his head. He grabbed the angry man's leg and pulled, and the man went down.

Jake felt the weapon connect with his ribs. Once. Twice. He grabbed for it, missed, and rolled aside as the club swung again and smacked the asphalt with a dull thud.

He felt his aching ribs. He would be okay. Fortunately, the attacker was on the ground and hadn't been able to wind up his swing; otherwise Jake might be lying beside Shaft, unable to move.

Jake scrambled to his feet in time to see the assailant straighten up, turn around, and run behind the next car, heading for safety, the weapon still gripped in one hand.

Jake followed, the pain in his side keeping him from making his best speed. He pulled out his cell phone and called 9-1-1 as he ran after the assailant. He gave his location and asked for an ambulance as well as a cruiser ASAP.

The attacker was fifty feet away, heading up beside the warehouse, but not gaining ground. Despite the ache in his side, Jake had stamina, and the man was tiring. It was just a matter of time.

They rounded the front of the building. Jake drew closer as the man dug in his pocket, removed a ring of keys, and slid to a stop beside a pickup.

Jake put on a burst of speed as the man hopped inside and slammed the door. The locks snapped shut and the vehicle roared as the engine caught. The truck began to back out.

Jake was too late.

No, he wasn't.

He dove the last few feet, leaped up, and landed with a thump into the back of the pickup.

If the guy was going to run, Jake was going with him.

The man turned and glanced through the rear window, his eyes wild, panic setting in. Surely he knew as well as Jake did, he wasn't going to get away.

The truck continued to back up, and then it stopped and spun forward, heading across the lot.

Jake could wait it out. The guy could run as far as he wanted to, but once he ran out of fuel, it would be all over.

But then, Jake had a better idea.

He crouched down and picked up a tire iron lying on the bed of the truck, hefted it in his hands, and struck the tempered glass of the rear window with the sharp end.

The driver and the front seat of the vehicle were sprayed with glass as the window shattered into a thousand pieces. The man hunched forward at the steering wheel, raising his arm as if to protect himself, but the vehicle kept moving.

Jake tossed the iron onto the bed of the truck, crouched down, and smiled in the rearview mirror at the man's frightened face.

"Maybe you should pull over," Jake said.

"Never."

"It might be safer." He raised his fists for the man to see. "When I wrap these around your neck and squeeze, not only will you get hurt badly, but I'm afraid your beautiful truck will be half-destroyed."

The man's eyes darted back and forth from the front window to the rearview mirror. Jake saw him weighing his options.

They neared the gate, when finally the vehicle slowed and stopped. The driver put the truck in park, dropped his hands to his lap, laid his head back, and sighed.

"Good choice," Jake said. "Now unlock the door and get out. The police are on their way, and if you surrender now, things might go better for you."

In perfect timing, a siren whined in the distance. The man flinched. It might be the ambulance, but the man didn't know that.

A few moments passed and no words were spoken, then the man reached for the door handle, opened the door, and stepped out as Jake jumped from the back of the truck.

"You're under arrest," Jake said. "Put your hands behind your back."

The man dropped his head and did as he was told.

Jake held the man's wrists together, gripped in one large fist, and marched him to the rear of the building.

Shaft was sitting up, leaning against his vehicle, a hand holding his ribs.

Jake turned his head as the ambulance pulled up, a police car not far behind.

Shaft looked up at Jake. "Thanks," he said grudgingly. "You might've saved my life."

CHAPTER 38

Thursday, 11:44 a.m.

ANNIE GLANCED at her watch. She had an appointment with the Nortons' next-door neighbor, Sharon Stipple, at noon and didn't want to be late. Sharon was a cashier at Mortino's, and Annie knew the manager of the large food mart was a stickler when it came to employees taking extended breaks.

She selected a leather satchel from a shelf behind the desk, slipped in the folder she would need, and snapped it closed. She hung it on her shoulder and, on her way through to the front door, grabbed her keys along with a small handbag from the kitchen counter.

On the phone, Sharon Stipple had seemed like a nice person, and though Annie had a few questions lined up, she planned to see where the conversation led and follow it.

When she pulled into Mortino's, the large plaza was as busy as usual, but she managed to get a spot close by the doors. She got out of the car and looked at her watch. It was 12:04. Sharon would be on her lunch break now.

She opened the front door of the food mart and headed toward the back of the store. She knew where the break room was. She shopped here often, and when she spied the manager coming toward her from the far end of the aisle, she paused and smiled.

"Good afternoon, Mr. MacKay."

Somewhat bowlegged with a slight limp, he favored his right leg as he walked toward her and stopped. "Afternoon, Annie," he said. He pushed his butcher cap back and rubbed his prematurely bald head. "How's Jake?"

"Jake is well." She paused. "I'm here to talk to Sharon Stipple for a few minutes." She smiled again. "She should be on break now. I hope you don't mind?"

MacKay glanced toward the rear of the store, then back at Annie, a barely perceptible frown on his forehead. "I guess a few minutes won't hurt."

"Thanks. I won't be long."

"Okay, take care," MacKay said, and waddled off.

Annie went to the rear of the store and stopped at an "Employees Only" sign taped securely to a swinging metal door. She pushed the door open and stepped inside.

Three people sat at a long table near the side wall. They leaned back, munching their meal, their eyes glued to a television hung in the corner. One was a young man, two were women. One of the women, a pleasantly plump young girl, waved a hand and sported an attractive smile. That must be Sharon Stipple.

"Sharon?" Annie asked as she approached her. The girl nodded, her smile remaining, and motioned toward the vacant end of the table.

Annie shook her hand, moved down the table, and introduced herself as they sat. Sharon laid her lunch on the table and ate while they chatted about the weather, Sharon's job, and the high price of groceries. The girl certainly loved to talk.

Finally, Annie moved the conversation toward the reason for her visit. "Sharon, I'd like to ask you about the Nortons. As you probably know, Michael Norton was found murdered yesterday and I'm investigating his death." She paused. "How well do you know them?"

The smile on the girl's pudgy face drooped. "So sad to hear about Mr. Norton. I've known him for a few years. They've lived there as long as I can remember. I didn't know him real well. We said hello sometimes, maybe chatted a bit, but he always seemed like a great guy."

"And Mrs. Norton?" Annie asked.

Sharon's eyes narrowed in thought. "Don't know her very well. I've seen her out the back, gardening, cleaning up, but we never really talked. Seems to keep to herself most of the time."

"Did you ever notice them together? How did they get along?"

Sharon shrugged. "I never noticed anything unusual."

"Never heard them argue?"

"No," Sharon said. She cupped her hands in her lap and cocked her head. "I talked to the police about this already.

They asked me the same question, but as far as I know, they got along okay." She shrugged. "I've never been inside their house, so I have no real idea about their relationship."

"I realize the police have talked to you," Annie said with a smile. "But if you don't mind, I prefer to go over it again."

Sharon smiled wide. "I don't mind. If you can find out who killed him, I'll do whatever I can." Her smile disappeared. "It's a real shame."

"Thanks, Sharon. I'm sure you realize how important this is."

"Absolutely."

Annie took a deep breath. "Michael Norton was last seen by his wife on Monday morning," she said. "Can you remember when you saw him last?"

Sharon thought a moment, her green eyes far away. Finally, "I think it was Sunday afternoon. He was mowing the front lawn. I was on my way to work."

"Did you talk to him?"

She shook her head. "Just waved. He waved back and that was it."

"And you haven't seen him since then?" Annie asked.

"No. That was the last time, as far as I can remember. I know I didn't see him after work that day."

Annie opened the satchel, removed a file folder, and laid it on the tabletop. She slipped out a photo and turned it around for Sharon to see. It was a red Ford pickup, the same as the truck Rocky Shaft drove.

"Have you ever seen a vehicle like this in their driveway?"

Sharon looked at the picture and shook her head dubiously. "I can't be sure. It doesn't look familiar."

Annie removed another photo. It was of Rocky Shaft. She held it up. "Have you ever seen this man at their house?"

Sharon leaned in and squinted. "I don't think so." She looked at Annie and giggled. "I don't usually pay a lot of attention, but sometimes they have guests over for a barbecue in the backyard." She looked at the photo again. "I'm pretty sure I've never seen him, though."

Annie put the photo back in the folder and slipped out a shot of Werner Shaft. "What about him?"

Sharon's eyes brightened. "I recognize him. He's been there before."

"Can you remember the last time you saw him?"

"Not sure. Maybe a couple of weeks ago. He was in the backyard having a beer with Mr. Norton and one other man."

"Was Mrs. Norton there?"

"No. Just the three guys." She paused and pointed at the photo. "Who's he? Is he important?"

"He's Werner Shaft. The man who was murdered Monday evening. Did you hear about that?"

Sharon caught her breath. "Oh. I heard about that. Did they find out who did it yet?"

"Not yet," Annie said. "The police are still investigating and so are we."

"So that's what this is all about," Sharon said.

Annie nodded, and then asked, "The other man in the backyard that day—do you know who he was?"

Sharon pursed her lips, shook her head, and spoke slowly. "No. That might be the only time I saw him there." She tilted her head slightly. "I hope you don't think I'm a nosy neighbor. I'm really not, but sometimes it's easy to notice little things like that."

"Of course not," Annie said, tucking the photos back into the folder. She flipped it closed, dropped it into the satchel, removed a business card, and handed it to Sharon. "You can call me if you think of anything else that might be important."

Sharon took the card, glanced at it, and smiled. "I'll be happy to."

"I'd better let you finish your lunch and get back to work before Mr. MacKay gets after you," Annie said as she stood. "I know what he can be like sometimes."

"He's okay," Sharon said. "I know how to handle him." She giggled. "His bite's not half as bad as his bark."

They said goodbye and Annie left the room, waved at Mr. MacKay on the way out, and went to her car.

The revelation that Werner Shaft and Michael Norton socialized on occasion was interesting. Though Tammy Norton claimed otherwise, Annie wondered if the woman was more aware of that relationship than she let on.

CHAPTER 39

Thursday, 12:54 p.m.

WHEN HANK AND KING returned to the precinct, they were notified of the arrest of Stanley Asher. According to the report, Asher had attacked Rocky Shaft in the parking lot behind Shaft's place of employment. Hank grinned when he saw Jake's name on the report.

A background check on Asher turned up nothing unusual—no criminal record, no prior arrests, and no pending warrants.

Hank let Asher stew in the holding cell while he went over his notes from the Harland Eastwood interview. It hadn't broken the case open, but they had gleaned some information about the heist.

He was convinced Eastwood told the truth when he said his boss had no idea who robbed them of their ill-gotten gains. Once this case was over and done with, the names of any surviving robbers would be made public, and Hank suspected there would eventually be repercussions. The drug lords couldn't afford to let that go—it was bad for business.

Hank pushed back his notes, stood, and turned around. King sat at his desk, his chair tipped back, one foot resting on the faux-oak top. King browsed some paperwork, and Hank was surprised to see him putting in some rare desk time.

"Let's talk to this Asher character," Hank said as he approached his partner.

King's chair dropped forward with a clunk and his feet hit the floor. He tossed the papers onto his desk, yawned, and stood. "He's in interview room one. I had him brought up a few minutes ago."

King led the way across the floor and down a short hallway to the interview room. An officer stood outside the door to make sure Asher stayed put. He nodded at the detectives and stood aside as they approached.

Stanley Asher sat at the metal table, gazing at his fidgeting hands. He glanced up briefly, a sullen look on his face when Hank pushed open the door and entered.

King stood and folded his arms, leaning against the wall, while Hank took a seat across the table from Asher, sat back, and observed the suspect.

Asher avoided Hank's gaze for a few moments longer as the cop sat in silence. Then the man's curious eyes turned upward and caught Hank's stare, and his hands became still.

"Why'd you attack Rocky Shaft?" Hank asked.

Asher dropped his hands to his lap, rocked back and forth in his chair, and remained quiet.

"Aggravated assault with a deadly weapon," Hank said.

"That's a serious charge." He leaned forward. "With the intent to cause bodily harm." Hank looked at King and shrugged. "Who knows? The crown might want to pursue an attempted murder charge."

Asher's eyes narrowed. "I didn't try to kill him. I only wanted to teach him a lesson."

"He's got a cracked rib," Hank said. "That's serious, and you could've killed him."

Asher gritted his teeth. "He murdered my cousin. Michael and I were like brothers when we were young. My parents took him in when his mother and father died. We practically grew up together."

King bounced off the wall. "That's a sad story." He leaned in. "Now, how do you know Shaft killed your cousin?"

Asher looked up at King. "I saw it on the news."

"There's no proof it was Shaft," Hank said. "You're looking at serious jail time for assaulting someone who might be innocent."

"Do you know Rocky Shaft?" King asked.

The suspect shook his head. "Never met him before."

"How did you find him?"

"It wasn't hard. His name and picture was on the news and I tracked him down."

"Tell me about Michael Norton," Hank said.

"What do you want to know? He's dead now. We've always been close, and even after we went our own ways, we still hung around sometimes."

"If Shaft didn't kill him, do you have any idea who else might've wanted him dead?"

Asher shook his head. "No."

King bent over the table. "You and Rocky Shaft were involved in a robbery a few months ago," he said. "Tell us about that."

Asher looked confused. "What're you talking about?"

"Norton was a criminal," King said as he straightened his back. "Are you telling me you didn't know about that?"

Asher hesitated. "I knew he went to prison a few years ago, and he might've been involved in some shady deals after he got out, but I wasn't part of it."

"What kind of deals?" Hank asked.

Asher licked his lips and looked at Hank. "Can you get my charges knocked down to simple assault if I tell you?"

"Depends on what you have. I can probably convince the crown to drop the attempted murder charges."

The suspect frowned. "I ... I don't want to go to prison."

"That might be up to Shaft. If he presses charges, you'll be lucky to get by with aggravated assault."

Asher rocked in his seat, rubbing his hands together. He sighed deeply, and then spoke. "Michael was involved in the heist you mentioned. He told me about it. I swore to keep quiet, but he's dead now, so you can't do anything to him."

Hank leaned forward and rested his arms on the table. "Who else was involved?"

"I ... I don't know. More than just him, but I don't know who."

"Where's the money?" King asked.

"I don't know. Why would he tell me?"

"I thought you two were close?"

"Sure, but … he didn't tell me, and I didn't ask."

King swung a chair over to the desk, flipped it around backwards, straddled it, and laid his arms on the back of the chair. He looked intently at Asher. "Who killed Werner Shaft?"

Asher shook his head and looked back and forth between the detectives. "I honestly have no idea. They said it was Michael, but I know it wasn't."

"How do you know that?"

"Because he's not a killer. He was a good guy."

"A good guy who robs people," King said dryly. "Don't forget, he was in prison for burglary."

Asher jutted his chin. "Yes, he was. But in all those cases, I'll bet you won't find one case where anyone got hurt."

"You seem to know a lot about his crimes," Hank said. "Except the one we're asking about. Why is that?"

Asher shrugged. "Everything I know is public information. I followed his case, and I was in contact with him while he was inside, but we never talked about what he did. And I know he never hurt anyone."

Hank looked at King and jerked his head toward the door. They stood and King followed Hank into the hallway.

"I think he's telling the truth," Hank said. "He's just a guy who decided to take matters into his own hands. It was a dumb move, to be sure, but I guess he figures blood is thicker than water."

King nodded. "Yeah, you might be right. I don't think he knows anything else."

"All right. Book him for assault, and at least he'll be handy if we need to talk to him again." Hank turned away and then stopped. "See if you can convince Shaft to let this guy off with simple assault. He doesn't belong in prison."

King went back into the interview room as Hank went to his desk. Asher had confirmed what Michael Norton admitted during his phone call to Annie—Norton was one of the three men who had committed the heist.

Asher also seemed convinced Michael Norton wasn't a killer. Hank wasn't so sure.

CHAPTER 40

Thursday, 12:51 p.m.

WHEN ANNIE ARRIVED home, Jake was lounging in the living room. She sat down and filled him in on her interview with Sharon Stipple. There wasn't much to tell, and soon the conversation turned to Jake's encounter with Stanley Asher. She was concerned Jake might be injured, perhaps a cracked rib, or worse.

"It's honestly just a bruise," Jake told her, sitting up to prove his point. "Shaft is the one who got the good beating. They took him to Richmond General, bandaged him up, and released him. He's got a cracked rib, and he'll be sore for a while."

"It's a good thing you were there," Annie said. "He might've been killed."

"Perhaps," Jake said. "But if I hadn't riled Shaft up, he might never have left the warehouse, and might never have been beaten."

Annie shook her head. "You can't blame yourself. Asher was out to get Shaft and he would've waited as long as he needed. Shaft should be thanking you."

"He did," Jake said. "And he sounded sincere."

"His life might still be in danger."

"From whom?"

"I don't know. If he's not the killer we're looking for, then he could be next."

"And if he is the killer?"

"Then we have to prove it," Annie said. "One thing I know for sure, he's involved in all this."

"I'd still love to find out where the money is," Jake said. "That's the key to it all."

"We'll find it. Somebody knows, and they're not going to leave it alone forever."

Jake shrugged. "I haven't ruled out Maria Shaft. If her husband knew where the money was, he might've told her. It might even be hidden in their house somewhere."

"The same goes for Tammy Norton," Annie said. "Although Norton claimed on the phone his wife knew nothing about it."

Jake glanced at his watch. "Let's see what's on the news."

Annie reached for the remote control and turned on the television. Channel 7 Action News was coming on and Lisa Krunk's face took up most of the screen.

"I've just received some breaking news," Lisa was saying. "Rocky Shaft, the chief suspect in the slayings of Werner Shaft and Michael Norton, was attacked this morning by an unknown assailant. I've been unable to obtain the name of his attacker, but Shaft received some injuries before the attack subsided."

"How did she hear about that so fast?" Jake asked.

"She has eyes and ears everywhere," Annie said.

A picture of Rocky Shaft appeared on the screen and Lisa continued, "Rocky Shaft was questioned by police earlier and released. Apparently, they didn't have enough evidence to hold him, but I'm told the case against Shaft is mounting, and it's just a matter of time until he's arrested and charged."

"Where did she get that?" Jake asked. "That's not even true."

Annie turned off the TV and laid the remote control on the stand beside her. "If Lisa can't dig up any sensational news, she makes it up." She stood. "I'll be in the office if you need me."

She sat at her desk, turned on her computer, and spread out her notes. She scrutinized every detail in an attempt to make some sense of what they knew. Finally, she replayed the phone conversation with Michael Norton.

No matter how she connected the dots, it all pointed to Rocky Shaft. But something didn't sit right with her. Something disturbed her about the obvious conclusion, and she couldn't put a finger on it.

If she had a way of knowing where Michael Norton had been when he'd called her, it might give her a lead.

She had an idea. She knew someone who might be able to help.

Better known by his friends as Geekly, Jeremiah Everest was a long-time friend of the Lincolns and helped them on occasion when they needed his expertise. When it came to anything technical or computer related, Geekly was the absolute best.

She duplicated the folder of recent phone recordings onto a flash drive and wrote a note asking Geekly to analyze the recording labeled "Michael Norton" for any background sounds or other information that might shed some light on the location of the caller.

She dropped the drive and the note into a padded envelope, addressed it to Jeremiah Everest, and called a local courier. She asked for same-day delivery and twenty minutes later the package was on its way.

~*~

HANK TURNED as Captain Diego poked his head from his office and motioned him over. "And bring King with you," he called.

Hank found his partner in the break room. "Diego wants to see us."

King tossed a half-eaten sandwich into a paper bag, balled it up, and made an expert shot into the wastebasket. He stood without a word and followed Hank to Diego's office.

Hank sat and leaned back while King took his usual spot, holding up the filing cabinet, his arms crossed.

"Fill me in on the Shaft case," Diego said, looking at Hank and smoothing down his black mustache.

"I'm afraid we haven't made a lot of headway," Hank said. "But we've confirmed the drug money heist was perpetrated by three gunmen. We're no closer to finding the killer or killers, but we're pretty sure it wasn't a revenge killing by the drug lords."

King added, "And the best motive we can find is the money from the heist."

"And that points to Rocky Shaft, does it not?" Diego asked.

"I'd say yes," Hank said. "But we don't have enough for a search warrant or an arrest warrant."

Diego steepled his fingers under his chin. "What about that character who beat up Shaft?"

Hank shook his head. "Stanley Asher. He's just a fool looking for revenge. I don't think he's involved in any other way. And he has solid alibis for both killings."

"But he also confirmed Norton was in on the robbery," King said.

Diego took his cap off, ran his fingers through his dark hair, and replaced his hat, adjusting it in place. "Any luck in finding the money?"

"No luck," Hank said.

"It seems to me," King said, "if Rocky Shaft killed his brother as well as Norton, he would make sure he knew where the money was hidden first. So whether or not he knew before that, you can bet he knows now."

"I agree," Hank said. "But with all this heat around him, I doubt if he'll go near it."

"He would if he thought it was in danger," Diego said.

"That's what Jake tried to do," Hank said. "Jake told Shaft he knew where the money was. Jake told me he was pretty sure Shaft was headed to check on it when he got waylaid by Asher."

"We've got a tail on him," King said. "Ever since he was released from the hospital, he's been watched. If he goes near the money, we'll get him."

Diego leaned forward. "That's all well and good, but I'm more interested in getting him for murder."

"So are we, Captain," Hank said. "But we have to find something on him before we can get a warrant to search his rooms. Everything we have is circumstantial."

Diego sat back, dropped his arms on the armrests, and blew out a long breath. "All right, guys. Get out there and find something. And keep me informed."

"We'll get him," King said as he straightened his back. "It's just a matter of time."

Diego waved them out and went back to his paperwork.

Hank returned to his desk, dropped into his chair, and sighed wearily. He wanted to get this case cleaned up before somebody else turned up dead.

CHAPTER 41

Thursday, 3:15 p.m.

LISA KRUNK HAD already convicted Rocky Shaft. As well as being, in her humble opinion, the best reporter this town had ever seen, she considered herself a first-class investigative journalist, yet to be nationally recognized, but unsurpassed in her chosen field.

She had everything it took—expertise, tireless perseverance, and a dogged determination. And with Don at her side, ready to capture telltale video and sound bites, she was always raring to go.

Recently, she had cracked a lot of cases wide open, and was confused she hadn't received the recognition she so richly deserved. Unfortunately, others always stepped in at the last moment to claim the accolades belonging to her.

But this time, things would be different, and she resolved to get to the heart of the killings she knew Rocky Shaft was responsible for.

Her sources had confirmed that Shaft had been released from the hospital and returned home to nurse his wounds. One way or another, she had to speak to him.

Lisa leaned forward in the passenger seat of the Channel 7 Action News van as she directed Don on the route to the Shaft residence.

She pointed. "Pull over there."

The van pulled to the curb. Lisa observed the house a moment and then jumped from the van. Don got out, slid open the back door, and removed his camera.

She passed the red Ford pickup parked in the driveway and trod the brick pathway to the front door. Don dutifully followed, always ready to shoot at her pleasure.

She rang the doorbell and waited. There was no answer, so she persisted, ringing again and again.

"Go away. I don't want to talk to you." It was a muffled voice Lisa recognized as Rocky Shaft's.

Lisa rapped on the door and raised her voice. "I want to tell your side of the story," she lied.

There were a few moments of breathless silence as Lisa's heart beat in anticipation. Then she donned her best smile as the security chain rattled.

"Get ready, Don," she said through her smile.

Don was poised and so was she. The door swung open a few inches, revealed a frowning face, and Lisa was ready. "Mr. Shaft, I'm sorry you were attacked. It was a senseless and cowardly thing to do, and I was deeply disturbed to hear about it."

The frown on Shaft's face lessened at her words. He held

a hand over his side and bowed slightly forward as if to lessen the discomfort. Lisa could see the bulky bandage under his thin shirt.

"May I talk with you for a few moments?" Lisa asked, her fake smile spread wide.

Another hesitation, then the door opened all the way and Shaft stepped onto the front porch. He turned to face Lisa. "I'll give you a few minutes."

The camera was recording, the mike was on, and Lisa spoke. "I hope you're not in a lot of pain, Mr. Shaft?"

"It's not so bad, but I find it hard to move around much."

"Did you know your attacker?"

"He said he was Michael Norton's cousin."

"Is he blaming you for Norton's murder?" Lisa asked.

Shaft glared at Lisa, an accusing look on his face. "He saw your newscast."

"I'm sorry he misconstrued my story. I assure you, I didn't intend this to happen."

A brief look of doubt crossed Shaft's face, then he said, "My brother and one of his acquaintances were murdered. You should be looking elsewhere for the killer."

Lisa wanted to be careful, not yet ready to make her accusations. She cocked her head, tried to look puzzled, and said, "There's a lot of evidence pointing toward you, Mr. Shaft. How do you respond to that?"

Shaft frowned again, a hint of anger. "What evidence?"

"There's probably nothing to it," Lisa said soothingly. "But your threat to kill Michael Norton might be seen by some as evidence of your involvement."

"I was angry," Shaft said. "He killed my brother."

"You have a record of assault. How do you answer that?"

Shaft sighed. "That was a long time ago and had nothing to do with my brother's murder."

"I'm sure you're right," Lisa said, smiling again.

"Of course I'm right."

It was time to ramp it up. Time for the big question. "Mr. Shaft, my sources have reported a rumor of a robbery you were involved in with your brother and Michael Norton. Can you confirm that story?"

Shaft's body stiffened at the question. "As far as I know, no such robbery took place." His face reddened. "My brother was an honorable man and I resent any accusations he was involved in anything criminal."

"He was in prison."

Shaft leaned in. "A long time ago."

Lisa tilted her head. "Do people change, Mr. Shaft?"

He leaned in closer, his nostrils flared, and he raised a fist. "People can change. People do change, and I resent your accusations."

Lisa moved back half a step. Don moved to one side and trained the camera on Rocky Shaft.

She spoke again, the smile long gone, replaced by a look of disdain. "Did you shoot your brother, frame Michael Norton, and then kill him as well?"

Shaft's eyes bulged, his face turned crimson, and his raised fist came over and knocked the microphone from Lisa's hand. It landed on the brick sidewalk with a clunk and rolled to the driveway.

Lisa stepped back against the brick wall of the house. Don leaped onto the front lawn, careful to keep the camera trained on the action.

Shaft moved in closer, his face inches from hers. From ten feet away, the microphone picked up his raised voice. "I want you off my property. Now."

Lisa didn't budge. She pushed her nose into the air and glared into his eyes. "Stand back, Mr. Shaft."

The pain in Shaft's ribs seemed to be forgotten and he reached up and wrapped both hands around her throat. He squeezed, not too tight, but Lisa found it hard to breathe.

"Get your hands off me," she managed to say.

He dropped his hands from her neck and grabbed her by the upper arm. "Get out of here," he said, pointing toward the street with his other hand.

She continued to glare, unmoving.

He tugged at her arm, swung her away from the wall, and pushed her sideways with both hands. She lost her balance, tottered a moment, then tumbled off the edge of the porch and landed in a heap on the grass at Don's feet.

The cameraman stepped back and kept the camera trained on Shaft as the angry man leaped off the porch and approached him. Don took another step back, then another, moving steadily toward the street while the red light glowed.

Shaft stopped and stood still, his fists clenched at his side.

Lisa scrambled to her feet and moved safely out of the way as Shaft strode back to the house, stepped inside, and slammed the door behind him.

She knew there was a constant threat of danger in being an

investigative journalist, especially a world-class one like herself, and she wasn't averse to receiving the occasional bruise for the sake of the story.

She was relatively unhurt, feeling triumphant as she walked to the van. Things had gone much better than she could ever have hoped for.

Don shut down the camera, tucked it safely into the back of the vehicle, and helped Lisa climb into the front seat.

He went around to the driver side, hopped in, started the vehicle, and pulled away from the curb as Lisa picked up her cell phone and called the police.

She had to report an assault.

CHAPTER 42

Thursday, 3:56 p.m.

HANK WAS TAKING a breather in the break room, trying in vain to enjoy a cup of some of the worst coffee ever made, when King poked his head through the doorway.

"Forensic report on Norton is in. You might want to see this. Some interesting stuff."

Hank jumped up, dumped the last half of the foul liquid in the sink, and went to his desk to join King.

He sat down, pulled up his chair, slid his copy of the report toward him, and flipped it open. "What's so interesting?"

"Second page," King said as he leaned back and stretched out his legs. "Near the bottom."

Hank flipped to page two and scanned the bottom half of the sheet. He sat forward. "They found yellow nylon rope fibers on both sleeves of Norton's shirt as well as minor bruising on his wrists, suggesting he might've been tied."

"Which means Nancy was probably right," King added. "Norton was sitting, maybe tied to a chair, when he was shot."

Hank looked at King and slapped the desk. "That's it."

King looked up from the report. "That's what?"

"The rope. I saw a yellow nylon rope in the back of Rocky Shaft's truck when I went to his house to interview him last night."

"You searched his truck?"

"Nope. It was in plain sight. I didn't touch a thing."

King sat forward and looked intently at Hank. "That might be enough for a warrant," he said.

"Should be. See what you can do. Get a warrant to seize Shaft's truck as well as for a search of the house. Make sure you include his lack of an alibi for the time of his brother's murder as well as for the time of Norton's murder. And mention the bank withdrawal. I don't want this to fail for want of evidence."

King stood and hurried to his desk. Hank knew King would have to fill out some paperwork, but the search warrant should be a cinch and not take long to process.

Hank studied the rest of the report. Nothing else was revealed that he hadn't already known or presumed.

He looked up when King approached his desk. "Got the paperwork done, but I just got some more interesting news." King grinned. "Shaft is cooling in a holding cell. He's been arrested for assaulting Lisa Krunk."

"Lisa Krunk?" Hank said. "Is she all right?"

"She's fine. No damage done. He probably hurt her pride more than anything else."

Hank laughed. "Lisa and Shaft are two people you don't want in a room together. That is, unless you want sparks to fly."

"You can bet Lisa egged him on," King said.

"I have no doubt about that."

King shrugged. "She might drop the charges. Knowing Lisa, she'll make a deal with him. She has it all on video, and I doubt if he'll be able to worm out of this one." He turned. "I'd better go," he said and strode toward the door.

Hank had a choice to make. Now that Shaft was in custody, he was free to question him as much as he wanted— unless Shaft asked for a lawyer. Or he could wait until the search of Shaft's truck was complete. Then he might have the heavy guns he needed to get a confession.

Half an hour later, King was back. A willing judge had signed the order, and the search would commence immediately. King had given the investigators instructions to make an inspection of the truck their first priority and report back to him ASAP.

"Let's talk to Shaft," Hank said. "If CSI finds what I think they're going to, it won't take them long."

Hank had Shaft brought up to the interview room. He gathered up the folders from his desk, and he and King went down the hall and entered the room.

Rocky Shaft scowled and glared up at Hank. "This is a load of crap," he said. "That woman pushed me too far."

"From what I understand, you're the one who did the pushing," Hank said as he took a seat and dropped the folders on the metal table.

"Sure, I did. But she's not hurt in the least. Maybe her pride, but I'm the victim here." Shaft leaned back, folded his arms, and shook his head in frustration. "Maybe you should arrest her."

"How are you a victim?" King asked, leaning in.

"She accused me of killing my brother."

"Did you?"

Shaft gave King a black look, then glared at Hank. "I can sue her for slander."

Hank shrugged. "That's up to you, but we can't arrest her for that. It's a civil matter and you'll have to work that out with your lawyer."

"I don't need a lawyer." He spoke in a loud voice, the extra effort causing him to hold his side and grimace. He was obviously in some discomfort.

"You might need a lawyer after this," Hank said. "If the crown pursues assault charges, they can do so without Lisa's approval."

"It's all bogus," Shaft said. He leaned forward and spoke in a calmer voice. "Can't you see that?"

"Maybe it is," King said. "But murder isn't." He paused as his cell phone rang. He pulled it from his pocket, looked at the caller ID, and grinned. "I'll be right back." He left the room, closing the door behind him.

Hank leafed through the folders as Shaft watched him curiously. Finally, the suspect spoke. "What's in those folders you keep looking at?"

"Evidence," Hank said.

"What kind of evidence?"

Hank didn't answer. He continued to study the papers as he waited for King.

Finally, the door opened and King stepped in. Hank saw the good news on the detective's face as he took a seat beside Hank, leaned forward, and placed his arms on the desk.

"Can you tell me how Michael Norton's blood got into the back of your truck?" King asked.

Shaft looked bewildered and he stared at King. "What're you talking about?"

King leaned in and pointed a finger at the suspect. "You murdered Michael Norton, dragged him to a spot by the railroad tracks, and dumped him there."

"And we have the rope," Hank said, looking at King. King nodded and Hank continued, "You tied him up and killed him. We found the rope in the back of your truck along with traces of Norton's blood."

Shaft narrowed his eyes. "What right have you to search my truck? You're making this all up."

"I'm afraid not," King said. "We got a warrant to seize your truck and search the house."

Hank picked up a sheet of paper from the folder. "You made a withdrawal for six thousand dollars cash from your bank account on Tuesday morning. We know the money was to pay off the hitman."

"You're both crazy," Shaft said. "I didn't hire a hitman and you can't prove otherwise."

"What was the money for, then?" King asked.

Shaft sat back, folded his arms, then winced and held his ribs. "It was to pay off a gambling debt."

"Can you prove that? Who'd you pay off?"

"My bookie. And no, I can't prove it."

"And you have no alibi for the time of either murder," Hank added.

"I told you where I was before."

"Yes, you did. When your brother was murdered you were home alone. And when Norton was murdered you claimed to be at a restaurant. We checked. Nobody remembers you there."

Shaft's eyes flared and he slammed a fist on the table. Then he closed his eyes a moment, took a deep breath, and spoke quietly. "I think I need a lawyer now."

CHAPTER 43

Thursday, 7:20 p.m.

JAKE FINISHED WIPING down the Firebird, pulled it into the garage, and shut the overhead door. He didn't like to leave his baby outside overnight; you never knew what the weather would be like.

He went through the door into the kitchen and found Annie at the table helping Matty with his homework. They were working on some math problems, and Annie was showing him how to figure out the answer without the aid of a calculator.

"I'm exercising my brain," Matty said. "Mom says it's important, and I guess she's right. It's a lot harder, though."

"Your mother's right," Jake said.

Matty yawned and faked a pout. "Are we done yet?"

"Just a few more," his mother said.

"How many's a few?"

Annie laughed. "Do three more. If you get them right then you can watch TV."

Matty sighed, his shoulders slumping, and chewed on the end of a pencil as he attacked the next problem.

The doorbell rang and Jake went to the door. It was Hank. "I'm on my way home," the cop said. "Thought I would drop by and see what's going on with you two."

"Annie and Matty are in the kitchen. Come on in," Jake said.

Hank followed Jake in, greeted Annie, and gave Matty a fist bump. "What're you working on there?"

"It's math," Matty said. "Boring stuff."

"Sure, it's boring," Hank said. "But when you need it, it can be fun."

Matty dropped the pencil and looked at Hank. "Fun? How?"

Hank laughed. "Okay. Maybe not fun, but useful."

Matty sighed and went back to work.

"Anything new with you guys?" Hank asked, looking back and forth between Jake and Annie.

"Not a lot," Jake said as he sat. "My ribs are feeling better." He touched his side and twisted in his seat to prove it. "I might be a little stiff in the morning, but I think I'll live."

"Can't say as much for Rocky Shaft. He's still in pain." Hank grinned. "Oh, by the way, we arrested him. Charged him with first-degree murder in the death of Michael Norton."

The Lincolns listened intently as Hank described the assault on Lisa and the discovery of the rope and blood in Shaft's vehicle.

"So that's it?" Annie asked. "You have it wrapped up?"

"Not quite," Hank said. "We still have nothing on him in the murder of his brother. It still looks like Norton killed Werner Shaft. I'm presuming Rocky Shaft then killed Norton in revenge."

"It's all too neatly wrapped up," Jake said, shaking his head. "I'm not so convinced Shaft is dumb enough to leave such damning evidence laying around."

"Frankly, I'm not convinced either," Hank said. "But we have no choice other than to follow the evidence."

Matty listened intently, twiddling the pencil between his fingers. "Did you catch a bad guy, Uncle Hank?"

Hank chuckled. "It looks like it, Matty."

Annie leaned forward. "Matty, finish your homework, please." She turned to the cop. "Hank, I went to see Sharon Stipple today. She's the Nortons' next-door neighbor. I showed her a photo of Werner Shaft. She told me she saw him having a beer with Norton in their backyard."

Matty's head was down, his homework forgotten as his wide eyes peeked up.

"We always assumed there was more to their relationship than their wives let on," Hank said. "It doesn't prove anything."

"It proves somebody's lying," Jake said. "If they lie about one thing, we can't believe much else they say."

"And what about the money?" Annie asked. "Any luck in finding that?"

Hank shook his head. "Rocky Shaft still denies all knowledge of it, and the other two are dead. It might never show up." Hank sat back and crossed his arms. "We had a tail on him until he was arrested, and he never made a suspicious move. And when they searched Shaft's apartment downstairs, nothing of interest showed up. No money. No weapons. Nothing."

"Just in his truck," Jake added.

"So if what you assume is true, and there's more to this than meets the eye," Hank said. "Who framed Shaft?"

"Maria Shaft? Maybe Tammy Norton, or how about the guy who cracked Shaft's ribs?" Jake touched his side. "And almost cracked mine."

"Stanley Asher," Hank said. "Nope. He's got a solid alibi for both murders."

"You've ruled out the drug dealers, Hank?" Annie asked.

"Not a hundred percent. But I can't find anything on them."

"I assume you still haven't located Norton's car," Jake said.

"Nope. When Shaft killed Norton—or whoever did, he disposed of it somewhere. So far it's eluded us."

"Something doesn't add up," Annie said. "If Shaft killed Norton, why'd he tie him up first? Why not shoot him on the spot?"

"He had to have been holding him for a while," Hank said.

"Why?"

Hank thought a moment. "Maybe so he could frame Norton for the murder of Werner Shaft before he killed him."

"If that's correct," Jake said, "and Rocky Shaft is smart enough to do all that, then his last stupid move was to leave evidence in his truck? Makes no sense to me."

Hank chuckled. "Seems like we've been over all this before, and yet the evidence circles back to Rocky Shaft. Don't forget, he's hotheaded, and he was stupid enough to assault Lisa Krunk. Perhaps his anger got the better of him more than once."

"Good point," Jake said, but he wasn't so sure.

Hank yawned and stood. "I guess I'll get going. I want to drop by and see Amelia for a while and then get to bed early. It's been a long day."

"See you later, Uncle Hank."

"Later, Matty."

Jake stood, saw Hank to the door, watched until the cop drove away, and then went back to the kitchen.

"Do you think this case is wrapped up?" Annie asked Jake as he sat at the table.

"I have my doubts."

"Me too."

CHAPTER 44

DAY 5 - Friday, 8:40 a.m.

ANNIE HUSTLED MATTY off to school, cleaned up the kitchen, and went into the living room to enjoy her second cup of coffee for the day.

She heard the Firebird roar in the garage, and the overhead door whined open. Jake was off to get something done to his car—she wasn't sure what it was and hadn't asked. The house was all hers for now and she intended to catch up on some reading.

She settled into the armchair, curling her legs underneath, picked up her book from the stand beside her chair, and opened it at the bookmark.

Lately she had been delving into the world of crime scene investigation, studying one of the many books on law enforcement that filled the bulging bookcase beside the fireplace.

Before she could finish the first page, her cell phone rang.

She tucked the bookmark back in, put the book in her lap, and looked at the caller ID. It was an unknown number.

She answered the phone. It was Tammy Norton returning her earlier call.

"I want to drop by your house if possible," Annie said. "I'd like to talk to you regarding Rocky Shaft."

Tammy hesitated. "How about right now? I don't have to be at work until this afternoon."

Annie told her she'd be there shortly and hung up. She had some pointed questions to ask, and was sure Tammy knew more about Rocky Shaft's involvement than she let on. Perhaps Tammy feared for her safety, but now that Shaft had been arrested and was almost certain to be convicted, her worries should be over.

She got her handbag and car keys from the kitchen, propped a note for Jake against the coffeepot, and hurried out to her car.

A few minutes later, she pulled to the curb in front of the Norton house and got out. She wondered who was responsible for taking care of the upkeep of this run-down property. It looked like it needed a thorough makeover.

Tammy's Ford Probe wasn't parked in its usual spot in the driveway. Annie assumed it was in the single-car garage attached to one side of the house.

She went up the pathway to the front porch and rang the bell. In a moment, Tammy opened the door, a pleasant smile on her face, and invited her in.

Annie stepped inside, followed the woman, and took a seat on the couch, laying her handbag beside her. She watched as Tammy sat in the armchair, leaning forward slightly, her hands in her lap.

Annie spoke. "How're you making out? I know this has been hard on you."

Tammy sighed. "Very hard, but I think I'll be okay." Her eyes roved around the room. "This place seems so empty without him, though."

"I know exactly what you mean," Annie said. "If you need anything you can always call me. Even just to talk."

"Thank you," Tammy said. "I might take you up on that. Things do get rather lonely sometimes. Especially lately." She sighed deeply and lowered her head. "I only wish things could've been different."

Annie looked at the young widow and felt compassion. It was always hard to find the right words at a time like this.

Dispensing with more small talk, Annie said, "I don't know if you've heard. Rocky Shaft was arrested last night."

Tammy caught her breath. "I hadn't heard." She narrowed her eyes. "He killed my husband. I know that. Is that what he was arrested for?"

Annie nodded. "They found some evidence. Enough to charge him with first-degree murder."

"That's a relief," Tammy said. "I don't know why it took them so long, but I'll be glad when it's all over. It's been a nightmare, that's for sure."

Annie smiled and looked at her handbag. Her cell phone was ringing. She smiled weakly at Tammy. "I should take this," she said. She removed her cell from her bag and looked at the caller ID.

It was Geekly. For him to call back so soon, he must have some good news for her.

"Hi, Jeremiah," Annie said. "I've been expecting your call."

"Greetings, Annie," he said. "It's good to talk to you again. How's Jake?"

"Jake's doing good." She looked at Tammy. "I'm with someone right now, so I don't have a lot of time to talk. I'll make sure to call you later." She paused. "Give me a quick rundown of what you found."

"Will do," Geekly said. "I had a chance to go over the stuff you sent me this morning and I have some interesting data to share."

"I assumed that."

"It's a good thing you labeled all the files," Geekly said. "It helped me keep everything straight."

Annie held up a finger toward Tammy and whispered, "I'll only be a minute." She spoke into the phone. "What did you find?"

"I think the most important thing is the recording of the phone call from Michael Norton to you."

"Yes."

"I know you only wanted me to analyze it for background sounds, but I noticed something peculiar."

"Spill it out, Geekly," Annie said.

"I did hear a background sound. It seemed to be a dog barking."

"A dog? I didn't hear a dog on the recording, and I played the call back several times," Annie said.

"It was faint and it took me some time to isolate it. But it didn't sound right. It sounded to me like a voice changer was being used. A voice changer can alter the pitch and timbre of the user's voice to either make them sound like someone else or disguise their voice and perform changes in real-time. So I adjusted the tone, pitch, and timbre of the recording using special software until the bark sounded normal."

"And?"

"And I ended up with a totally different voice."

Annie gasped.

"I got curious, so I compared acoustic patterns and speaking style using a series of verification processes and pattern-matching algorithms and found a conclusive match on one of the other recordings in the folder you sent me."

"Yes?"

"The voice on the recording matched the file named 'Tammy Norton.'"

Annie swallowed hard, finding it difficult to breathe. "Thanks, Geekly. That's all I need for now." She paused and thought quickly. "Let Jake know the news." She hung up the phone slowly. Her heart pounded against her ribs, her throat was dry, and her hands trembled.

The truth was hitting her, and hitting her hard. If the phone call hadn't been from Michael Norton, but rather from Tammy, then everything on the call was a lie. Everything had been staged for her benefit. There could only be one reason for the deception—to throw suspicion onto Rocky Shaft.

And away from Tammy Norton.

That meant Tammy was aware of the robbery and might even have been part of it.

And that meant Tammy Norton might've killed either her own husband, or Werner Shaft—or both. It was the only thing that fit.

She was sure now. Tammy Norton had killed Werner Shaft, framed her own husband for the murder, then killed him and framed Rocky Shaft. It was foolproof, except for one thing. Tammy didn't know Lincoln Investigations recorded all phone calls in and out of the office landline.

Tammy eyed her curiously. "Is everything all right?"

"Yes. Everything is fine," Annie said, faking a smile.

"You don't look so good."

"May I use your washroom?" Annie asked. She had to get away and call 9-1-1. She couldn't do it in front of Tammy. The telltale tone of the emergency phone number would be recognized by anyone.

Tammy motioned toward the hallway. "Down there. Second door on your left."

Annie tucked her cell phone into her handbag, picked up the bag, and stood. "Thank you. I'll be right back."

She hurried in the direction Tammy indicated, opening the second door. She stopped short and frowned. It was a bedroom. Had Tammy suggested she use a washroom in the master bedroom? She took a step inside and stopped. Surely she heard wrong. There must be another washroom.

She stepped back into the hallway, spun around, and stared open-mouthed into the muzzle of a pistol pointed toward her head, Tammy Norton's leering face directly behind.

CHAPTER 45

Friday, 9:29 a.m.

ANNIE GLARED INTO Tammy Norton's eyes—eyes as cold as the steel gripped in the killer's hand. The woman handled the gun expertly; it was obvious she'd done this before. She was a killer, and would have no hesitation to kill again.

"You know, don't you?" Tammy said, her voice unemotional and lifeless.

"Know what?"

Tammy sneered. "Don't pretend to be stupid. I heard the phone call and I know what you talked about. It's unfortunate for you that you got involved in all this."

Annie raised her chin and remained silent as she fought to still the trembling inside.

"Why didn't you just leave it alone?" Tammy's brow tightened. "Why'd you have to push it when you already had your killer?"

Annie matched the woman's gaze, remaining quiet and unmoving. Finally, she spoke. "I wasn't convinced."

"The police are convinced. Rocky Shaft killed my husband and the evidence against him is overwhelming. I made sure of that."

"Yes, you did," Annie said. Her eyes moved to the weapon, then back to the killer's face. "It was brilliant, a perfect plan, until you called me pretending to be your husband."

"That should've worked. In fact, it did work. It had you all fooled, but sadly, I never thought you might record the call." Tammy shook her head, her lips tight. "That was my only mistake, but it's still something I can overcome."

"The police will figure it out eventually," Annie said. "And Jake will too. And when he does, he'll track you down like a dog and you'll be finished."

Tammy gave a short laugh. "Perhaps he will, but we won't be around if he does."

"Where are we going?"

Another short laugh, then, "You'll see. I'll come up with a plan. Something to cover me." She laughed out loud. "I can either frame you, or make you disappear forever. Or both."

"You tried that already," Annie said. "With Punky Brown."

Tammy sighed deeply. "Punky Brown. That was my last dumb move." She chuckled. "Hiring a punk to take care of something I should've done myself. After that fiasco, I resolved to do my own killing in the future."

"The police have the recording."

"But they won't have me." Tammy smiled with her lips but the ice remained in her eyes. "And if you disappear as well, who's going to know the truth?"

"You might kill me, but they'll find you."

Tammy's eyes glimmered. "I have half a million to keep me company and keep me hidden for a good long time. It's not hard to buy a new identity and start a fresh life elsewhere. It's a big country."

"It's greed that got you into this and it's greed that'll get you caught. You have the robbery money, don't you?"

Tammy drew herself up and sneered. "Of course. Who do you think ran the whole show?" She rolled her eyes. "Do you think I would trust those bozos to do what only I could do?"

"So you double-crossed them. You used them to do your job for you, then killed them because the money got to you."

Tammy shrugged. "I got tired of waiting, and frankly, I got tired of them." Her eyes glazed and she motioned with the pistol. "Enough talk. Time to go."

Annie didn't move. "What about Rocky Shaft? He knows what you did."

Tammy laughed, long and hard. "Rocky Shaft knows nothing. The poor sap was in the right place at the right time to fall neatly into my plans." Tammy's face grew cold and her eyes tightened. "After I got rid of his brother, the idiot came to me with some story about his brother and my husband committing a robbery. He wanted to cash in on his brother's share. He didn't know I was the boss and I didn't tell him. But that's when I saw him as the perfect patsy." She shrugged and grinned. "And my plan evolved from there."

Annie knew she was up against a cold-blooded killer who would do whatever it took to get what she wanted. Annie also knew she had some time to come up with a plan of her own.

The killer wasn't going to shoot her here. That wouldn't fit in with her scheme to make Annie disappear and make a clean getaway.

"It's time to go," the killer said, waving the gun again. "Back up. Into the kitchen."

Annie adjusted her handbag, turned slowly, and walked down the short hall and into the kitchen. She stopped and waited, trying desperately to come up with some means of escape.

The back door was dead ahead. Maybe she could make a run for it. She looked to her left. The kitchen circled back around to the living room. Could she take a chance? She shuddered at the thought of a bullet entering her back as she run. No. That wasn't the answer.

"You don't need this anymore," Tammy said, pulling the handbag from Annie's shoulder. Annie turned her head and watched as the woman dug around inside the handbag, removed her cell phone and car keys, and handed the bag back. "We can't leave this lying around, can we? You'd better take it with you."

Annie put the bag over her shoulder, her mind still in turmoil as she tried to devise a way out.

Tammy took a step back, kept one eye on Annie, and fiddled with the cell phone with her free hand. "There," she said at last, holding up the phone. "Just in case you're wondering, I turned off the GPS. Unfortunately, I'll have to discard this thing once we get out of here."

"Where are we going?" Annie asked.

"You'll see." Tammy backed to the counter, picked up a

key ring, then moved back and opened a door. She waved the pistol. "In there."

Annie turned and looked through the doorway leading into the garage. Tammy's dark blue Ford Probe was parked inside. The barrel of the pistol pressed into her back as Tammy prodded at her from behind. A beep sounded as she stepped into the garage and the trunk lid of the Ford popped open.

Annie considered swinging her handbag in an attempt to catch Tammy unawares and maybe disarm her. The killer would be nothing to handle without her weapon, but the woman seemed to be quite capable with it. It was a dangerous plan, and Annie decided to wait for a more opportune moment.

"Get in the trunk," Tammy said, standing well back and motioning toward the vehicle.

Annie looked at the open trunk, glanced across the darkened room toward a door leading to the outside and freedom, and hesitated.

"Get in," the killer repeated. "You won't get away through there. I'm an expert shot and you wouldn't get halfway to the door before I kill you."

Annie crossed her arms and glared at Tammy. "Where are you taking me?"

Tammy's eyes narrowed, a sneer appeared on her lips, and she thrust the gun two inches closer. "In."

Annie gave her captor a black look, then climbed into the trunk, turned onto her back, and lay still. Tammy's smug face disappeared from her view as the trunk lid slammed, leaving Annie in total darkness.

CHAPTER 46

Friday, 10:11 a.m.

WHEN JAKE ARRIVED home, he was surprised Annie's car wasn't in the driveway. He knew she had called had Tammy Norton earlier, requesting an interview, and he assumed that's where she was.

He pulled the Firebird into the garage and revved the engine a couple of times before turning the key off. He went into the house, peeked into the office, then dug out his iPhone and sent her a text message: "Home now. Miss you."

When he didn't get a return message, he assumed she was deep into the interview. The text tone sounded on the phone as he was pushing it back into his pocket. It was Annie: "Miss you too. See you soon."

He wandered into the kitchen to find something to soothe his growling stomach and saw a note from Annie propped up against the coffeepot. She was at Tammy's. No surprise.

He made a cup of coffee, found a leftover chicken

drumstick in the fridge, and sat at the table, enjoying his snack and sipping coffee.

When he finished, he put the dishes in the sink and looked at his watch. Unless something else came up, Annie should be on her way home now. He called her number and it rang several times before going to voice mail. She was probably on the road. His wife was a stickler for not talking on her cell while driving. It was a habit he had yet to break.

After a few more minutes, he tried her number again. There was still no answer and he began to be concerned. This wasn't like Annie.

Jake booted up the "Find My iPhone" app but Annie's cell location didn't show up. He frowned at his phone. Something didn't make sense. Why would she turn the GPS off?

He stood and paced the floor when another call went unanswered. Something was wrong.

His phone rang and he looked at the caller ID, hoping it was Annie.

It wasn't. It was Geekly.

"I can't talk now," Jake said, answering the phone. "I'm trying to find Annie."

"That's why I'm calling," Geekly said. "I talked to her a little while ago and gave her some interesting news regarding the file she sent me." He paused. "But something she said bothered me, and I started thinking about it. Before she hung up, she said, 'Let Jake know the news.' It didn't make a lot of sense at the time, but in hindsight, she seemed a little nervous on the phone. I thought I'd better call you."

Jake stopped pacing. "Where was she at the time?"

"I don't know. She said she was with somebody."

"Yeah, she was with a woman named Tammy Norton," Jake said. "But I can't reach her on the phone."

"Tammy Norton?" Geekly said. "That's strange."

"In what way?"

"I gave Annie all the technical details, but the gist of it is, when I dissected the call from a guy called Michael Norton, it turned out to be Tammy Norton's voice disguised as his."

Jake sprang to his feet. "Are you sure about that?"

"Absolutely. I'll explain it to you if you want."

"No. Never mind. I'm sure you're right." Jake took a deep breath, his eyes narrowed and unfocused. Annie wasn't answering her phone, and Tammy Norton wasn't the innocent victim she claimed to be. That could only mean one thing.

Annie might be in danger.

"I have to go, Geekly," Jake said suddenly. "Annie's in some trouble. I'll call you." He hung up and ran into the office. He leafed through Annie's notes, found Tammy Norton's phone number, and dialed. He paced uneasily and waited, but there was no answer.

He dialed Hank's number, ran to the kitchen for his car keys, and was in the garage before the cop answered the phone. "Annie's in trouble," he said into the phone as he jumped in the car and started the engine. He gave Hank a quick version of the story while he waited impatiently for the garage door to open.

"I'll send a pair of cruisers immediately and meet you there," Hank said. "But don't go near the house until the officers get there."

"I'll be careful," Jake said, and hung up.

The Firebird roared from the garage and spun onto the street. He didn't know what he would find at the Norton house—maybe nothing at all, but he was determined to find out ASAP.

As he neared the house, he expected to see Annie's vehicle parked at the road. It wasn't there.

He pulled into the empty driveway, raced from the vehicle, and went to the side of the garage. He peeked through a small window in the outside door. His heart jumped when he saw Annie's vehicle inside. That was a dead giveaway. Something was definitely wrong.

It was a single-car garage, and Tammy Norton's dark blue Ford was nowhere to be seen. Tammy was gone. But where was his wife?

He hurried to the front door and banged furiously as two police cruisers pulled to the curb. Four officers streamed from the vehicles. Jake knew what their instructions would be. Enter the premises by force, if necessary, find Annie, and apprehend Tammy Norton.

As two officers ran to the back of the building, Jake stepped away from the front door as the other two cops raced to the front porch.

"Police. Open the door."

The door remained closed, and then burst inward as the second cop hit it with a battering ram. The officers moved in cautiously, their weapons drawn, ready to bring them into use at a moment's notice.

Jake turned as Hank pulled into the driveway behind the Firebird and jumped out. "Is she here?" Hank called.

"It doesn't look like it." Jake shook his head grimly. "The officers are inside, but I think both women are gone."

"Stay back," Hank said as he drew his handgun and stepped into the house.

Jake followed Hank and stood in the foyer. The officers were busy, clearing the house, room by room. Before long they approached Hank. "No one's here," one of the cops said. "And there's no sign of a struggle."

Hank's face was grim as he pulled out his cell phone. "I'll get a BOLO out on Tammy Norton's car immediately."

Jake raced frantically around the rooms, through the kitchen and the living room, and finally to the garage. He pulled on the door handle of Annie's car. It was unlocked, and the keys were in the ignition. He checked on the floor, the backseat, and the front seat, but nothing appeared to be out of place.

As far as he could tell, Tammy Norton had kidnapped his wife. He had to do whatever it took to find Annie. He prayed she was still alive.

If what he assumed about Tammy was correct—that she was a cold-blooded killer—he knew there would be no negotiations, no ransom, and no mercy shown.

CHAPTER 47

ANNIE GRIPPED THE wheel wrench firmly in both hands as she waited for the trunk lid to open. During the long ride to wherever they were now, the heavy bar was the only thing she could find that made a suitable weapon, and she planned on giving it her best shot.

She hadn't considered the possibility that Tammy was the ruthless killer she'd turned out to be. And all because of money. She hoped Geekly had understood her message and that Jake and the police were searching for her. She had no idea where she was, but if the building they were in was connected to Tammy, the police might be able to put the pieces together. She hoped they'd figure it out before it was too late.

The car stopped and she heard the unmistakable hum of an overhead garage door, then the vehicle moved ahead several feet.

She heard the same hum as the door closed, and then the car engine died. A vehicle door opened and slammed shut, and then footsteps came closer. She gripped the wheel wrench, readied herself, and waited.

The trunk lid popped up and her only chance of attack faded. Tammy stood well away from the trunk, the pistol in her hand.

"I thought you might try something like that," the abductor said. "You can drop it now."

Annie considered her situation for a brief moment before letting the iron slip from her hands. It made a dull thud as it hit the floor of the trunk.

Tammy stepped back and waved her weapon. "You'll be happy to hear we've arrived at our destination. You can get out now."

Annie swung one leg over, then the other, climbing from the trunk. She stood upright and glanced around. They appeared to be in a garage attached to a residential house. The usual items that could be seen in most any garage were scattered about. Shelves contained a variety of containers, clutter, and castoffs. Garden tools occupied a bin on the floor. The rafters held more junk.

To her left, a door led into the house. Directly in front of her was an outside door. What were her odds?

Probably nil.

"Don't try anything stupid," Tammy said. "I could as easily shoot you right now, but if you're careful, you might live a little longer."

Annie crossed her arms and glared. "You aren't going to

get away with this, so you might as well shoot me now. What're you waiting for?"

Tammy shrugged and gave a fake smile. "I haven't figured out how you're going to fit into my plans. So you might be pleased to learn, until I do, you're safe with me." She laughed. "As long as you're a good girl."

"What is this place?" Annie asked.

"You don't need to know that. Just do as you're told." Tammy pulled a ring of keys from her pocket, selected one, and then moved to the door leading into the house. She unlocked it and pushed it open, then stepped back and made a sweeping motion toward the doorway. "Inside."

Annie glared at the heartless killer a moment longer and then took the two steps up, through the doorway, and entered a small foyer. She felt the cold steel of the pistol at her back and knew making a run for it was out of the question. Tammy wasn't taking any chances and neither was she.

The house had the feel of being lived in. She saw a kitchen off to her left, a short hallway leading to the front room to her right. Except for the pounding of her heart, the house was still and quiet.

"Open the door in front of you," Tammy said from behind.

Annie looked straight ahead. She knew where the doorway must lead—most certainly down to the basement.

It did. When she opened the door, she saw a flight of wooden steps leading into darkness.

Tammy reached to the wall beside the doorway and flicked

a switch, flooding the basement with light. The pistol prodded Annie forward.

"Downstairs. Move it."

Annie took the first step cautiously, her mind whirling in an attempt to devise a way out of this deadly situation. But Tammy was cautious. The woman stayed well back as Annie descended the stairs, the gun now prodding the back of her head.

Thirteen steps down and Annie touched the cold concrete floor. She looked around. The basement was almost empty, as though its owners had just moved out, or perhaps new ones about to move in. A furnace sat silently in the far corner, waiting for winter. An empty set of shelves stood to her right, more to her left.

Across the room, near a darkened window, sat a lone chair, remnants of yellow nylon rope still clinging to the wooden arms, another short piece kicked to one side. Still more was coiled into a ball.

Someone had been tied to that chair recently and Annie knew who it was. Tammy Norton's own husband had surely been held in this very room until the unfeeling woman had seen fit to work him into her plans, resulting in his brutal death. And then the scheming woman had planted a piece of the rope in Rocky Shaft's vehicle along with blood from the victim.

And now, Annie was headed for that same fate, one she was determined not to submit to.

The killer pushed Annie forward, then stepped aside and pointed to the chair. "Sit there," she demanded.

Annie sat, her arms on the armrests, looking up at the unfeeling woman.

"It'll soon be over," Tammy said, a smirk on her face.

Annie glared defiantly. "It'll soon be over—for you."

The woman laughed. "I doubt if you'll be so brave when the end comes." She picked up the coil of rope and peeled off several feet, being careful to stand well back from her captive, the gun never wavering. "Wrap your arms behind the chair."

Annie did as she was told, and the woman moved behind, tying the cord firmly to both wrists, and then to the chair. The cord bit into Annie's wrists and made her shoulders ache.

Tammy wrapped the stout cord around Annie's chest and the back of the chair several times, tying it in a solid knot to each armrest.

The ball of rope rolled and spun, unraveling from the coil as Annie's ankles were tied firmly to the chair legs. The rest of the cord was wrapped around and around, until finally, Tammy knotted the tail and stood back, smugly admiring her work. "That should hold you long enough."

"It should hold me until the police come," Annie said. "And then you'll be the prisoner."

Tammy gave a short laugh. "I admire your pluck, but unfortunately you're dead wrong. The police have no clue what's going on. All their efforts are aimed toward that poor sap, Rocky Shaft."

"We'll see," Annie said.

"Oh. And I sent your husband a text message before I

trashed your phone. I assume he was happy to hear you were fine and on the way home."

Annie's face flushed with anger. The woman was devious and covering herself well.

Tammy took a step back. "You can scream all you want once I'm gone. Nobody will hear you." She stepped to the bottom of the stairs and turned back, her foot on the first step. "I shouldn't be long, and you'll be safe here until I return."

Annie watched the woman climb the steps and the door at the top of the stairs closed. A lock slid into place and she was alone.

The room was still, and only the sound of Annie's breathing disturbed the deathly quiet that surrounded her.

CHAPTER 48

Friday, 11:15 a.m.

JAKE STOOD IN THE living room of Tammy Norton's house and stared out the front window, deep in tortured thought. All around him, investigators studied, photographed, and documented every detail of the house. Everything would be closely scrutinized and examined.

Hank and King were undertaking a thorough search in other rooms, hunting for evidence pointing to the location of the fugitive. Citywide, patrol officers kept a watch for all dark blue 1996 Ford Probes in an effort to apprehend the kidnapper.

Tammy's face would be shown on every news broadcast, part of the exhaustive search now underway.

The woman would be caught. Jake had no doubt about that, but with Annie as a hostage, he was in anguish over the possible outcome.

Jake turned from the window as Hank came into the

room. The cop's face was somber as he shook his head slowly. "Nothing turned up," he said. "King is still searching."

Unsure what to say, Jake took a deep breath and exhaled slowly.

"I'm convinced Rocky Shaft is connected to this somehow," Hank said. "I'm going to the precinct, and I'll give him a good grilling. He might know where Tammy Norton is headed."

Jake nodded. It seemed like a long shot, but at least it was something.

Hank touched Jake's arm. "Do you want to come with me?"

"I think I'll stay here. See if I can come up with an idea."

Hank turned to leave. "I'll let you know if I get something solid."

"Thanks," Jake said as Hank hurried toward the door. The cop disappeared outside. Jake turned back to the window and watched as Hank ran to his vehicle, jumped in, and set the portable flashing lights on the roof of the car. The siren sounded as he pulled from the curb and sped up the street.

Jake rubbed his hands through his hair and sat on the edge of the couch. If Tammy had fled and taken Annie with her, then his wife was probably still alive, and would be as long as her abductor found her useful. Jake shuddered to think what might happen at that point, but he was hopeful of finding her in time.

But time is useless without a plan, and Jake found it difficult to come up with a clue as to where to start looking first. He felt helpless in a hopeless situation.

King was in the living room now, rummaging through the papers in a desk beside the fireplace. Jake went over and stood beside the desk, watching.

"Just looking for any idea where Mrs. Norton is," King said without looking up. "She might be holding Annie hostage somewhere." He pulled out a drawer and examined some file folders closely, then rifled around in the top drawer, filled with pens, paper clips, and knickknacks.

"But if she doesn't know we're onto her," Jake said, "she might not be so careful. I hope she has no idea they're looking for her vehicle."

"Let's hope you're right," King said as he closed the final drawer and straightened his back. "There doesn't seem to be anything helpful here."

Jake left the room and went into the hallway. Investigators worked in the kitchen, the bathroom, and the bedroom, their faces grim as they went about their painstaking task.

Jake's cell phone rang and his heart missed a beat. It was Annie! "Where are you?" he almost shouted.

"Hello?" came an unknown voice from the phone.

Jake's heart dropped. It was a man's voice, speaking low and hoarse.

"Who's this?" Jake asked.

"It's Bob. Bob Langley," the gravelly voice said. "I saw someone toss this phone into a dumpster."

"A dumpster?"

"I was going to keep it. It looks to be in good shape, but I got to thinking, so I called the first speed dial number and here you are."

Jake's mind whirled. "Where are you?"

"Just off Main Street, near Lexington."

"Stay where you are. I'll be right there," Jake said as he raced for the front door. "Can you do that?"

"Sure. I guess so."

"I'll meet you on the corner of Main and Lexington."

"Okay. I'll be there," the man said.

Jake hung up and jumped into the Firebird. He had no idea if this would lead anywhere, but it was something at least, and he had to pursue it.

Lexington was about a mile north of his current location, in the heart of the suburbs. As he approached the intersection, he saw a man leaning against a light post. That had to be him. He ground the Firebird to a stop and wound down his window. "Bob Langley?"

The man nodded. "You the guy on the phone?"

"Yes. Show me where you found the cell?"

The man shrugged and pointed down the street. "Big blue dumpster behind that building."

"Which way did the car go after?"

"Back toward Main," Bob said. "I didn't see which way it turned after that."

"I need the phone," Jake said, holding out a hand.

Bob handed it over. "Any reward?"

Jake dug out his wallet and pulled out a twenty. "Here you go," he said, handing the bill to Bob.

Bob took it, folded it once, and tucked it into his shirt pocket. He smiled and stepped back. "You take care now."

Jake pulled from the curb, turned down Lexington, and

spun in behind the first building. A big blue dumpster stood against the building wall.

Was Annie close by, or had the woman dumped the phone and continued north? That was a question he couldn't answer.

He jumped from the car, ran to the dumpster, and looked inside. It was almost empty.

Jake jumped back in the car and drove up and down the surrounding streets, straining his eyes, looking for Tammy's car. Eventually, he gave up in disappointment. It could be anywhere in the city—or miles away by now.

He sat off Main Street for a few minutes and watched the cars go by, hoping he would see Tammy's vehicle, but knowing in his heart it was long gone.

Jake gave Hank a call. The cop answered, still in the middle of questioning Rocky Shaft. Hank wasn't ready to drop the charges against Shaft yet; they still had no hard proof against Tammy, but in light of the latest events, both Shaft and his lawyer were more accommodating.

"Shaft still denies involvement in the robbery," Hank told Jake. "But he admits he went to Tammy after the death of his brother, confronted her about the money, and claimed Michael Norton had killed his brother. He assumes that's when Tammy got the idea to frame him."

"If he wasn't involved in the robbery, then who was the third person?" Jake asked. "Maybe Tammy herself?"

"It's starting to look that way," Hank said. "According to Harland Eastwood, who I believe was present at the time, the gunmen wore masks."

"My only concern right now is Annie," Jake said. "Does Shaft have any idea where Tammy could've taken her?"

"He claims not to know and I believe him," Hank said. "He wants Tammy Norton found as badly as we do. That's the fastest way, and maybe the only way, to prove his innocence. I'll keep on him awhile longer and see if he knows anything else. In the meantime, cops all over the city are looking for Tammy's vehicle." Hank paused. "Hang in there, Jake. We'll find her."

Jake hung up the phone. He hoped Hank was right, because right now, he didn't know what else he could do to find his wife.

CHAPTER 49

Friday, 11:57 a.m.

ANNIE SAT QUIETLY in the chair, listening to the sound of her own breathing. She heard Tammy upstairs, her footsteps playing a soft staccato on the floor above as she moved about.

The woman must be planning something, or perhaps she was on the phone. Annie couldn't be sure, but she thought she'd heard a raised voice on occasion; now, though, only silence came from above.

Then a muffled car engine sounded, probably from the garage. In a few moments, the rumble faded away.

Tammy was gone and Annie was alone.

It had been necessary to wait until her abductor left, and now was the chance Annie had hoped for.

When Tammy had prodded her into the basement earlier, Annie had spied the coil of rope on the floor beside the chair and known what it meant.

When the kidnapper had wrapped the rope around her chest, Annie had held her breath as deeply as possible, tightened her shoulder and chest muscles, arched her back, and hunched her shoulders forward. It was difficult to maintain that position, but she'd persevered.

When her abductor had finished tying her to the chair and stood back, Annie had let her breath out carefully, keeping her muscles tensed.

After the kidnapper had left, Annie had relaxed and drawn her shoulders back, and the rope around her chest slacked by almost three inches. Her hands and feet were still tied tightly, but it was a start. And now that her abductor had left the house, Annie was about to see if her scheme would work.

Her plan was to grasp the rope about her chest with her teeth and gnaw her way through like a squirrel, but gravity took over, making the loosened cord loop downward, impossible to reach.

But this was a life-or-death situation—her life, or her death, and there had to be a way.

She came up with a dangerous plan.

She rocked the chair, back and forth, slowly at first, and then it gained momentum. She held her head forward to lessen the impact when the chair finally toppled backwards. It helped, but the back of her head hit the concrete and stunned her.

She took a few deep breaths and waited for her head to clear, then heaved her hips upward as far as she could. Gravity again took over, but this time, as she continued the motion, the rope eased its way toward her waiting teeth.

The nylon rope was tough and unyielding, but it was no match for her will. The woven strands broke loose one by one, until finally, the ends fell free.

Still a long way to go.

She listened for any sound from upstairs, but all was quiet.

Her legs were next. They were tied to the chair, but with the rope now slackened, it was an easy task to arch her back and slip them off the end of the chair legs.

She rolled to her side and struggled to her feet, standing at an awkward angle. Her hands were bound to the back of the chair, but now she could move them enough to work at the knots.

The nylon cord clung stubbornly to itself as she fought with it. Then finally something slipped and she got a better grip. She continued her battle with the rope until it fell away, the chair tumbled loose, and she was free.

Almost.

She still needed to get out of this room, the stairs leading up to freedom the only way.

She touched the back of her head and looked at her fingers. There was no blood. She had a mild headache, and the spot that struck the floor was tender to the touch, but she shook it off and concentrated on her escape.

Annie was almost certain Tammy had driven away earlier, but she wouldn't bet her life on it. She crept up the stairs and sat on the narrow top step, her ear to the door. There was no sound.

She tried the door handle. It turned but the door wouldn't budge, locked from the other side.

She leaned back and struck the door with her shoulder. It rattled and stayed solid. She held her breath, listening for signs of anyone in the house, but heard nothing.

Her continued effort to break the door down was getting her nowhere. There was no room to stand on the upper step and it was impossible to strike the door at the height of the lock using her shoulder. There must be a better way, and she needed to find that way before Tammy came back to finish what she started.

Annie ran down the stairs and looked around frantically, searching for something she could wedge into the lock, or anything that would serve as a battering ram.

The shelves were flimsy and useless. The other junk lying around wouldn't help. The only possibility was the chair. She hefted it. It was sturdy and might be of some use, but it would be awkward to handle in the confined space at the top of the steps.

She lifted it over her head and brought it crashing down, again and again, until finally the legs loosened and she wrenched them free.

Then the rungs at the back received the same treatment until she held only the solid seat in her hands.

She raced up the stairs and pounded at the lock with the makeshift battering ram. The frame splintered. She paused to catch her breath before continuing. Finally, the lock gave and the door popped open.

She tossed the seat down the stairs, took the final step into the foyer, and dashed to the kitchen. A phone rested on the counter. She picked up the receiver and put it to her ear.

There was no dial tone; the phone was disconnected.

Annie raced for the back door, flipped the lock, and pulled the sliding door open. She dashed into the bright sunlight, spun around, and saw a house to her left, another to her right.

She went left, ran up the side of the house where she had been held prisoner, then jumped a hedge to the front lawn of the neighbor's house.

She pounded at the door, keeping an eye behind her in case Tammy returned. She had no idea if anyone was home, but she knocked again.

Finally, the door opened a few inches, stopped by a security chain. A wrinkled face sporting a curious look appeared in the crack. The old man had a sparse covering of snow-white hair and he cupped a hand behind his ear. "Whatever is the matter?" he asked.

"I need to use your phone. It's an emergency," Annie said, a pleading look on her face.

The man stared a moment, a faint frown taking over his brow. He looked Annie up and down and then closed the door. The chain rattled and the door swung open.

"I guess it'll be okay," the old man said as he stepped back and waved her in. "Martha don't like anyone tracking about the house, but she ain't here right now and you sure look like you been through something."

Annie stepped inside. "Thank you."

The man pointed down the hallway. "Go on into the kitchen there and help yourself. It's hangin' on the wall."

CHAPTER 50

JAKE LOOKED AT his cell phone and frowned. It was an unknown number. He answered it, tucked it between his shoulder and ear, and put his hands back on the steering wheel.

"Jake Lincoln," he said into the phone.

"Jake, it's Annie. I'm okay."

Jake's heart jumped and he brought his left hand up to the phone, leaning forward in his seat. "Where are you?"

"At the north end of the city, near Main and Broad."

Jake looked in the mirror, touched the brake, and pulled into the left-hand lane. "I'm on my way," he said as he pulled a U-turn, heading back the way he'd come.

Since Jake had last talked to Hank, he'd been driving around endlessly, looking for Tammy Norton's car in the area where Annie's cell phone had been found. He wasn't far from her, and he listened while Annie gave him her exact location.

"I'll be there in five minutes. Don't go anywhere." He hung up, touched the gas, and swerved around a slow-moving vehicle.

Four minutes later, he pulled up in front of a small clapboard house and looked around for Annie. She streaked out from behind a thick bush, opened the door, and got in.

"Am I glad to see you," she said.

Jake grinned and leaned over while Annie kissed his grin. "Me too," he said. "What happened?"

The grin vanished from Jake's face, replaced by a worried look as Annie told him in as few words as possible how Tammy had abducted her and how she'd escaped.

"Did you call the police?" Jake asked.

"Not yet. I called you first." She reached for Jake's phone and called Hank. Whenever the detective was available, going through him was always the fastest way to get things moving.

"Hank will be here in a few minutes," she said after she spoke to the cop and hung up. "He's sending some cruisers as well."

Jake explained about Geekly's call, the search of Tammy's house, and how Annie's cell phone had been recovered.

"She has to get rid of my car," Annie said. "She might've returned to her house to get it."

"And when she finds a house full of police, and cruisers all over the street, she won't stick around."

"Exactly," Annie said. "Then she'll have no choice. She'll return here to finish me off."

Jake glanced through the windshield, then in the rearview mirror. "We should get this car out of sight in case she comes back. We don't want her to know you escaped."

He pulled from the curb, spun around, and drove to a side street. They got out and worked their way back, stopping beside a massive oak tree across the street from the house.

Jake kept an eye in the direction he expected Tammy Norton to come from. "Do you know whose house that is?" he asked.

"I didn't stick around long enough to find out. The phone was disconnected, and it seems to be vacant for one reason or another, although it's still full of furniture. It's been empty awhile, because she held her husband here before she killed him."

"She planned it well," Jake said.

"Almost well enough."

Jake took a step back and grabbed Annie by the arm, pulling her toward him. "I think she's coming."

A dark blue car came down the street. Jake squinted out from behind the tree. "It's her."

The Ford slowed and turned into the driveway. The garage door wound upward, the car pulled in, and then the door closed.

Jake looked up and down the street. The police were nowhere in sight.

"She's going to find out pretty quickly I'm gone," Annie said. "As soon as she gets in the house, she'll see the broken door."

Jake looked at Annie in alarm. "And then she'll run, and they might never find her."

Annie glanced at the house then back at Jake. "We have to stop her." She looked thoughtfully toward the house. "I think she has a plan. Someplace to go where it's safe after she leaves here. She might disappear forever."

Jake ran the options through his head. They could go into the house and hope to overpower her. That was dangerous. She was armed. They could wait for the police. Not a great option. Maybe they could follow her in the Firebird. Not such a great plan, either.

He looked at Annie. "Any ideas?" He could almost see Annie's mind at work.

"If we can't stop her," Annie said, "maybe we can slow her down."

"How?"

"Get your car," she said, turning and racing toward their parked vehicle.

Jake followed her, and they reached the Firebird and hopped inside. He started the car, the tires squealing as he spun it around.

Annie sat forward in the front seat and pointed. "Drive to the house."

He hit the gas, and the car surged forward and then slowed as he neared the house.

"Pull into the lane and park against the garage door."

Jake frowned.

"It won't hurt your baby. Just touch the door gently and stop. That'll keep it from opening."

Jake wasn't keen on the idea but it was a good plan. He pulled into the driveway, eased forward, and stopped, the front bumper firmly against the garage door.

"We'd better get out of the car," Annie said, opening the

door. "She's going to be as mad as a hornet when she finds out."

"Odds are, when the door doesn't open, she'll come out the back door of the garage to see what the problem is."

"Or maybe she'll try to ram it."

That worried Jake. If Tammy tried to force her way through when the door didn't open, it could cause damage to his vehicle. But it would be a small price to pay to capture a killer—one who had threatened his wife.

"Okay. We've slowed her down," Jake said. "Now what?"

"We hope the police get here soon," Annie said. "I'm fresh out of ideas."

Jake glanced down the street. There were no cars around. It had been several minutes since he called Hank, but the cop was nowhere in sight.

He pulled out his cell phone and called the detective. "Where are you?" he asked when Hank answered.

"I'm about five minutes away," Hank said. "I don't know how close the cruisers are, but I told them to leave their sirens off. We don't want to warn her."

Hank chuckled when Jake told him what they'd done to slow her down. "Get out of sight," Hank said. "We'll take care of her."

Jake hung up and spun around as an engine sounded from inside the garage. Tammy was leaving. The garage door motor hummed. The door shuddered and shook as the motor howled and worked uselessly. The door scraped up an inch and stopped. The motor died, then started its persistent whine again.

Annie followed Jake and they jumped the hedge onto the neighbor's lawn and crouched down out of sight. They watched as Tammy came from behind the garage, brandishing a pistol in one hand. She stopped short when she saw Jake's car in the driveway.

The killer spun around, glancing in all directions, her face flushed with anger. Then she opened the driver-side door of the Firebird and looked inside, probably hoping to find the keys in the ignition.

She slammed the door and looked toward the street, her brows in a tight, angry line.

Jake knew Tammy had no way out except by foot. He looked around anxiously for Hank as the killer tucked the pistol into her waistband and started off on a steady jog down the street, moving away from where the Lincolns watched helplessly.

CHAPTER 51

Friday, 12:45 p.m.

ANNIE WATCHED THE woman who had kidnapped her and threatened their lives disappear down the sidewalk. She was getting away.

"We have to follow her," she said, looking at Jake. "Or she might be gone forever."

Jake frowned at Annie a moment, then nodded and stood to his feet. "Stay behind me," he said, leaping into a jog.

"Wait," Annie called. "Give me your keys."

Jake stopped, turned back, and frowned as Annie caught up to him. "What for?"

"I'm going to cut her off. I think I know where she's headed."

Jake dug in his pocket, pulled out his key ring, and handed it over, a reluctant look on his face. "Be careful."

"Follow her," Annie said, pointing up the sidewalk. "Don't worry about me."

"I'll call Hank," Jake said. "I'll stay on the line with him until he gets here."

Annie turned and raced back to the Firebird, hopping in. She had only driven the powerful machine a couple of times in the past. Usually, she let Jake do the driving, or used her own little Escort.

But today, there was no choice.

The engine roared when she turned the key. She dug for a lever below the seat, tugging it forward to accommodate her normal legs rather than Jake's long ones.

The garage door shuddered and thumped as she put the vehicle in reverse and backed up carefully. She gave it a spurt of gas and the car leaped back, faster than she expected, and she was on the street, facing away from the direction the killer had fled.

She knew Tammy would be desperate now, and desperate people do desperate things. The woman was in a panic, with no choice but to get out of the subdivision and get to Main Street as fast as possible.

At least, that's what Annie was counting on.

Even at the rate Tammy was running, it would take her several minutes. Once there, Annie was afraid the killer would try to hijack a car. And if Tammy found herself cornered, it might end up as a hostage situation. That would put even more people in danger and must be avoided at all cost.

Annie needed her plan to work.

She spun the wheel, worked the car into low gear, and touched the gas, glancing in the rearview mirror as the car jumped forward. She saw Jake's back, now almost out of view.

She clung to the steering wheel, managed to find second gear, eased the clutch out, and took a quick right-hand turn without slowing down.

A cruiser breezed past. At the speed she was going on a residential street he undoubtedly would've pulled her over under normal circumstances. But today, she was sure the pair of cops inside the vehicle were intent on apprehending a killer, a little too late to do any good.

Main Street wasn't far ahead. She counted on a modest flow of traffic in this part of town during the day.

Annie was familiar with the streets in the neighborhood; in fact, her knowledge of the city could put any taxi driver to shame. She planned to use that knowledge now.

She touched the brakes lightly, slowed at a stop sign to avoid a pedestrian, and then swung onto Main. She spun the steering wheel to the left, cut to the inside lane, and whipped around a slow-moving vehicle. She was making good time and expected to have time to spare—but not much. Every second could count.

Her destination lay just ahead—just a few more moments.

Annie pushed in the clutch, hit the brakes hard, pulled to the curb, and stopped. She turned off the engine, leaving the key ring dangling from the ignition as she jumped out and raced toward the corner of the next street.

She stopped outside the doorway of a flower shop, two feet from the corner of the building. If she had judged this right, her quarry would appear directly in front of her shortly.

She eased to the corner, chanced a quick peek around, and then pulled her head back.

The killer was coming, working her way up the sidewalk toward Main Street. Her pace had slowed, she was tiring, her head drooped from exhaustion, but she would be here in a few seconds. Jake was nowhere in sight. Annie suspected he was behind, staying well out of the woman's view.

Annie bent her knees slightly, braced her feet, tensed her leg muscles, and waited.

The moment Tammy Norton came into view, Annie leaped forward and broadsided her, bearing her to the sidewalk. Tammy fell hard onto her back, caught by surprise and momentarily stunned, allowing Annie to straddle her.

Annie attempted to hold the killer's arms down, but Tammy wrenched one free and reached to her back, going for the weapon. Annie grasped the deadly woman by the wrist, and the pistol spun across the sidewalk, out of reach.

Tammy lay on her back and clawed like a wildcat, snarling through gritted teeth as she scratched and scraped to break loose from Annie's grasp. There were no rules as the battle continued. The killer raked at Annie with her nails, and heaved from side to side in a desperate attempt to free herself.

Three or four pedestrians gathered to watch and cheer, not making a move to retrieve the weapon or aid in the struggle.

The killer outweighed Annie by a good twenty pounds, and the element of surprise was gone, but Annie held on. She must persevere until Jake arrived.

Each of the combatants was filled with a determination of her own—the killer to escape, Annie to stop a cold-blooded murderer.

Tammy's longer arms reached Annie's throat, and her fingers tightened in a death grip. Annie fought for air, struggling to loosen the clutching hands.

From the corner of her eye, Annie saw Jake, fifty feet away, tearing up the sidewalk. In a few more seconds, it would be all over.

Then with a desperate move, the killer released her grasp on Annie's throat, heaved and rolled to one side, broke loose, and dived for the weapon. Annie came to a crouch. Tammy spun back, resting on one knee, the pistol in her hand.

The killer gritted her teeth. "Stay there or I'll kill you now."

Annie spread her arms in surrender and rose slowly to her feet, taking a step back. Off to her right, Jake came to a quick stop. "Tammy Norton," he called.

Tammy spun in his direction and came to her feet, the pistol gripped in both hands, her eyes sighting down the barrel. "Stay back," she screamed. "I'll shoot both of you and I won't miss."

One onlooker fled, the other two backed off, while still others gathered from a safe distance.

Annie's back was to the street, the possibility of innocent bystanders behind her. She took two steps to the right, a brick wall now at her back, as the killer spun toward her.

"Put the gun down, Tammy," Jake said.

Tammy glanced frantically in Jake's direction and kept the weapon trained on Annie.

A moment later, a brown Chevy squealed to a stop on the other side of the narrow street. Hank sprang out and came to a shooting position, his weapon in his hand.

"Police. Drop the gun!"

Tammy whirled to face Hank, her weapon poised, desperation now in her eyes.

Hank sighted carefully. "Drop the gun or I'll shoot."

The killer held the weapon firmly in both hands as she circled, training the gun on Annie, then Jake, and finally back to Hank. Her eyes flared red, her face flushed with anger.

Hank took a careful step forward, his eyes on Tammy's face, his weapon never wavering. "It's over. Drop it now before somebody gets hurt."

Tammy stared wild-eyed down the sights toward Hank, her jaw clenched. Then her finger tightened on the trigger and she dropped to a crouch, a shot exploding from her weapon.

Hank dropped at the same moment and fired once.

An onlooker screamed as Tammy's arms fell to her side and her eyes bulged. The gun slipped from her hand, bounced on the concrete, and remained still. The killer buckled to the sidewalk beside her weapon.

Annie dashed over, kicked the gun aside, and knelt down beside Tammy. She looked into the face of the killer, the woman's cold, hard eyes now softening, then slowly glazing over, then closing as the last breath escaped from her lungs.

Hank's shot had found its mark. The hole through the killer's heart ensured she would kill no more.

EPILOGUE

Friday, 4:40 p.m.

JAKE SIGNED HIS NAME at the bottom of his statement and turned to Annie. She had finished with hers some time ago and now leaned back in her chair, her eyes closed, waiting patiently for Jake.

"Done," he said, picking up Annie's statement and scanning it. Annie opened her eyes and sat forward as Jake shuffled the two pages together and handed them to Hank.

The cop looked up from his mound of paperwork, took the statements from Jake, and added them to his stack.

"Paperwork always ensures an exciting case comes to a tedious close," Hank said. "Sometimes it takes longer to document the case than it took to solve it."

Jake grinned. "That's what you get for being a cop. We're not hampered by such mundane details. A quick police statement, fill out an invoice, and case closed."

"And you're not hampered by having to shoot anyone,"

Hank added. "That always makes the wrap-up twice as painful."

"And twice as sad," Annie said. "It was unfortunate Tammy was too stubborn to surrender, even when she knew she couldn't win."

"Suicide by cop," Hank said. "To some, it's the easy way out of an impossible situation. Rather than face life in prison, they choose to end it all."

Hank looked up as King strolled over to the desk carrying Annie's handbag. "That suits you well," Hank said with a chuckle. "You should get yourself one."

King ignored Hank and gave the bag to Annie. He held up a digital recorder and handed a sheet of paper to Hank. "Here's some more papers for you, Hank. I had Annie's recording transcribed."

Hank took the transcription, scanned it, and whistled. "It's all here," he said, looking at Annie. "Tammy's complete confession. That was quick thinking in a desperate situation on your part."

"How'd you manage that?" Jake asked.

Annie shrugged. "After Geekly called me, I put my cell in my handbag and flicked the recorder on. Tammy took my cell phone, as you know, but missed the recorder, so I pumped her for as much information as I could get. Then I hid it in the trunk of the car for safekeeping, and there you have it."

"That'll save me a lot of headaches pinning all this on her," Hank said. "And it should clear Rocky Shaft of murder charges."

King laughed. "And to show you that bad guys finish first,

the crown isn't going to charge Shaft for assaulting Lisa Krunk."

"I suspect that's because they have a weak case." Hank chucked. "And the fact Lisa has been none too kind to law enforcement in the past might have something to do with their decision."

"You're probably right," King said. "And Lisa won't pursue charges because she made a deal with Shaft for his complete story and an interview."

"So everybody wins," Jake said.

"Everybody but the dead people," King said, leaning on the edge of the desk and crossing his arms. "Forensics is still going over the car, but so far, they found blood stains in the trunk, and I'm sure when it's analyzed, it'll prove to belong to her husband."

"I'm not sure if there's any way to prove it," Hank said thoughtfully. "But I suspect the bruises on Tammy Norton were not because her husband beat her, but rather from a life and death struggle with him."

"Did you find out who owns the house where she held Annie?" Jake asked.

Hank shuffled through the papers and withdrew one. "The Nortons were housesitting for a family on a European vacation. She took the liberty of using it as a safe house, so to speak."

"And where's the money?" Jake asked.

Hank shrugged and looked at King. King shrugged back. "It might turn up in the search of Tammy's house, but who knows? It could be locked away in a safe deposit box somewhere."

"I bet Rocky Shaft would love to get his hands on it," Annie said.

"It might never show up," Hank said. "But if it does, it'll be confiscated."

Jake looked around the precinct. "I hope it's found. You guys could use a few upgrades in here. Half a mill might get you a new desk, Hank."

The cop laughed. "I'd be happy with a new chair." He cocked a thumb over his shoulder. "Maybe we could replace that useless air conditioner over there."

Jake stood. "If we're done here, I have a very important client I need to see."

"What is it this time?" Hank asked. "A smuggling ring, or maybe international art thieves?"

"Something more important," Jake said. "I have to find a lost dog."

###